The Summer of Crud

Jonathan LaPoma

ALMENDRO

ISBN: 978-0-9988403-2-1

Illustration by Cinyee Chiu
Interior design by Polgarus Studio
Author photograph by Emilio Azevedo

For more information, contact info@almendroarts.com.
www.almendroarts.com
www.jonlapoma.com

Praise for *The Summer of Crud*

"A rollicking, entertaining adventure on the open road starring two ferocious youths fueled by booze, pot, and canned spaghetti . . . A slender, fast-paced, fever-dreamed excursion that . . . becomes undeniably addictive."

-Kirkus Reviews, Recommended Book

"Like a bad trip—filthy in all sorts of ways, yet weirdly endearing."

-Yuliya Geikhman, *US Review of Books*

"I couldn't help but recall my first impressions of Journey to the End of the Night by Louis-Ferdinand Celine . . . We see past the golden sunlight to the street kids with their broken dreams, to the panhandling in the Haight and the ghost of Kurt Cobain haunting the streets of Seattle . . . Danny's odyssey, his metaphorical Summer of Love, is both marred and enhanced by the reality of his physical condition and that of the world. At once unworldly and preternaturally wise, he sees past the trappings into a reality that is not entirely unexpected considering his life up to that point . . . the reader can't help but hope he will survive all he's experiencing . . . most highly recommended."

-Jack Magnus, *Readers' Favorite*, 5 Stars

"Unique . . . extraordinary . . . A pot-smoking, paradigm-changing journey that brings readers along for a wild ride, offering a high-octane blend of psychological revelations and cultural observation . . . especially recommended for readers who appreciate coming-of-age stories beyond the usual teenage angst focus."

-Diane Donovan, *Midwest Book Review*

"Twisted enough to be intriguing, but not so much that it's a turnoff . . . A deep, unique, extremely well-presented narrative of self-awareness while declining into mental illness."

-Book Bangs

"Not a light read . . . LaPoma paints a gritty picture of struggling young adults, living moment to moment, overwhelmed by adulthood. Dan's demons are present on every page and readers that suffer from anxiety or depression are likely to connect with his struggle for belonging and self-acceptance . . . Dan's inner voice speaks loudly to the difficulty many face on life's winding road."

-Red City Review

"A classic story destined to find its home in reading groups across the nation."

-Lisa McCombs, *Readers' Favorite*, 5 Stars

"Disturbingly deep, hypnotizing . . . the sort of writing that is book club worthy. I couldn't stop reading it even if I wanted."

-Atiqah, *Bookmarks & Blue Light*

"Definitely weird, but enjoyably so . . . A daring piece of work."

-Marjorie H, *Books & Tea Cups*

"Though The Summer of Crud is short, MAN is it deep! This narrative is chock full of harsh observances of human nature and insecurity . . . One of those books that is so full of incredible quotes that rather than sharing a few I might as well just give anyone a copy of the book and say "Here, read this; I really love it . . . like The Perks of Being a Wallflower's grungy older brother."

-Audrey L, *Netgalley Reviewer*

"Takes adventure and art to a whole other level . . . packed with life, lessons and realism. He gets into some deep shit and it will hit you . . . Even though it's from a man's POV, as a woman I completely understand and am sympathetic from a different aspect . . . it really reached a part of my soul that's hard to get to . . . You have to read this . . . There will be at least one chapter in here that will make you think . . . why is this so me?"

-Ash the Bookworm

To Paul Bern

Oh, lovely burden!
The sadness
Of the world
Is in my hands.
What shall I do
With it
Tonight?

Chapter 1

My phone rang at four twenty-three a.m. We'd planned to leave at seven. I should have known. "Yo, I'm in your driveway. Get your shit and get out here."

"Wha—? Okay, okay, I'll be right down." I got out of bed, threw on some clothes, and grabbed my flask, backpack, guitar, tent, and the rest of my gear. I walked outside, where Ian was standing beside his car.

"Fuck, how much shit are you bringing?" Ian said. "You're gonna have to put at least half of that back."

"I stripped it down to the essentials like you said."

"I already got a tent, and it's the fuckin' summer, man. You don't even need a sleeping bag."

"I don't know . . . I've heard it gets cold up in the mountains, even in the summer."

"Just leave it. Your guitar too."

"Isn't that the point of this trip?"

"There's no space."

I peered through the back window of Ian's aging Toyota Camry. "There's tons of space. Pop the trunk."

"My shit's already in there."

"Just pop it."

"Fine." He did and I checked it out.

"There's a ton of space in here too. It's just the two of us, man."

"My car's old. It'll never get us over the Rockies with all this weight."

"My tent and sleeping bag can't possibly weigh more than five pounds combined."

"Ditch the tent."

"You gotta be kidding me."

"I'll take off without you."

"Fine." I left the tent on my front porch and brought my sleeping bag, backpack, and guitar over to the trunk. He slammed it shut before I could put anything inside.

"It's already full."

I tossed my gear in the back seat instead and hopped into the passenger seat. Ian popped in his Cure CD and put on "Boys Don't Cry." We took off.

"Why'd you come so early?"

"We need to get rolling."

"Why?"

"Yo, if this is how you're gonna be this whole trip, I'm gonna leave your ass at the first gas station."

"Fine, fuck it."

We cruised down my street and made our way first to the 290, then the 90, and headed southwest around Lake Erie bound for the Great West. Bound for freedom. Buffalo was dark. But soon there'd be light.

We'd graduated from college a month earlier, and the road was calling us. We didn't have any specific plans, only a rough idea of where we were going: across the US to the

Pacific, then down to Mexico, stopping to see friends and national parks along the way. Other than to get out on the road and make some music, we never really discussed what we were looking for. But I figured Ian was searching for the same thing I was: something lost. Something buried way deep down. The Spirit of the Sixties. Peace. Love. Freedom of expression. The completion of all our half-written melodies. I wanted to write songs and play them on the streets of the Haight. I wanted to walk the alleys where Jack Kerouac and Allen Ginsberg passed bottles of port while waxing poetic. I wanted to strip down and run screaming through endless green meadows cut through with crystal-clear mountain streams. I wanted to roll in the dirt and wash myself in the rain and touch the earth and feel my atrophied spirit rise inside of me. America as I'd known it was oppressive and filthy and imbalanced and negligent and abusive. But there had to be a real America out there. A Great America. And there had to be a real me out there too.

But given how it started and all I knew of Ian and this world, I should have known our trip was doomed.

"I say we just keep cruising 'til we hit up Ricky's," Ian said.

"How far is that?"

"MapQuest said it's like ten hours to Normal, but we can make it there faster. I wanna get there by lunch."

The morning was dark, cool, and lonely, and we were pretty much alone on the thruway. The light, however, was starting to rise above the horizon. I sat back and tried to let the tunes take me, but the chemicals were raging, and my mind and body were both strangled up—muscles so tight, I felt deformed. I felt panic coming, but I'd felt panic my whole life and knew how to kill it away. But you've never taken a trip like this, Danny. You've never been stuck in a car for months. Stuck in a car with a lunatic, who, if he smells your panic, will do whatever he can to drive you over the edge. Stuck in a car where at any point one of *their* songs can come on the radio, and you'll be trapped. Kurt Cobain, Scott Weiland, Layne Staley. The voices of the Devil. The voices that haunted you during the Evil Times. Just one song can bring those horrific thoughts back, and where will you go now? No other distractions. Just endless road.

But it was that same endless road that had always soothed me. On the road, I could outrun the horror and inch closer to some miraculous place where the water tastes like wine and the climate suits my clothes. And I knew that's what awaited me at the end of this line. I knew it. It had to be. The songs couldn't be wrong. The songs had saved me. The songs had given me hope, a map to a better life. A map to the songs inside of me, burning for release. And if I had to hitch a ride with a lunatic to get there, then so be it. . . .

We stopped for gas and I took over driving.

"Ricky said he's got some bomb herb we can buy," Ian said.

"Fuck, man, I don't have much cash."

"Well, I'm out of that Da-Wayne."

"Dwayne's got the best shit. You just get this intense but mellow high without the fear and all that. I always get the best ideas and see the best colors on his shit."

"Well, this'll be some Midwest shit, grown in the soil that's fed this country for the last few hundred years. It'll probably be good too."

"I hope so, man. I want this trip to be perfect. Hey,

we should work on 'But I Gave It Away' while we're headin' over."

"Fuck that. You gotta be in the moment to write, and this ain't any kinda moment."

"It's just as good as any other."

"Naw." Ian turned up the song: "Everyday Is Like Sunday." Fucker loved him some Morrissey.

Music and motion. No talking. Just the pleasant hum of the road.

We breezed through Pennsylvania but hit a snag in Ohio. Even though I wasn't going that fast, a cop started following us, then after a few miles put on the lights. I figured he must've seen Ian drinking a beer and now we were both fucked. I pulled over, rolled down the window, and the prick approached. Ian killed the beer and slid the can under his seat.

"G-good morning, Officer," I said.

"License and registration."

"What's the . . . uh . . . matter?" I said.

"License and registration."

Ian reached into the glove box and handed over the documents. "It's my car. I was feeling a little tired, so he took over driving."

The cop went back to his car. He returned a few minutes later and said to me, "I'm gonna need you to step out of the vehicle."

"What for?" I said.

"Get outta the vehicle, son."

I opened the door and he directed me to stand with my arms raised and legs spread. "Now, if I pat you down, I'm not gonna find nothin' on you, am I?"

"No, of course not."

"WHAT!"

"I . . . I said no."

He started patting down my left leg. "Will I find anything in here?"

"No."

"WHAT!"

"No! No!"

He did the same with the other leg and both arms, then ordered me to walk to his car. "Get in."

The driver's side door was open, so I started for it.

"No, the back." He opened the door, and I got in.

He poked around Ian's car for a few minutes, then returned to his cruiser and sat in the driver's seat. He punched some shit into his computer without saying anything. The backseat was hard plastic and the radio blasted some country crap.

"Hey, can you turn this down?" I said.

"WHAT!"

"The music. It's killin' me, man."

He turned it up, then turned around. "Now, I'm gonna ask you a question, and I want a straight answer. Where are the drugs in your friend's vehicle?"

Thank god Dwayne hadn't come through. "Oh, there aren't any drugs in there."

"You sure?"

"Yeah, I swear to god."

"Now why would you go an' do a thing like that?"

"Like what?"

"Don't you dare bring jesus into this."

"Christ, look, there're no drugs. No drugs."

"I saw bits of marijuana in your lap."

I started laughing.

"WHAT!"

"I was eating a cookie. You probably just saw crumbs."

He punched some more shit into his computer, and I kept getting visions of him driving me out to a field where his buddies were waiting to beat on the hippy kid from New York. My mind was already twisted up and that was sure to do me in, but the fucker let me go with a stern warning to "avoid drugs at all costs."

Thanks for the advice, dipshit.

I got back in Ian's car and took off, following the speed limit all the way through the state.

By the time we got to Indiana, I was feeling better. Most beginnings were messy, whether in relationships or conversations or road trips, and I knew shit would balance out. We cruised past Illinois State University a little after one. Ian called Ricky to get directions to his place, and we arrived minutes later. He and Ian had studied geology together at Conesus, and Ricky hopped right into his master's program after graduating. Fuck. . . . Everybody seemed to know where they were going: full-time jobs or internships or grad school. Ian and I had been in a band that broke up about a month before graduation, and all I wanted to do was make music and keep rolling down the highway.

"Damn, that was fast," Ricky said as he approached the car.

"It's a fuckin' Camry, man," Ian said. He unlocked the trunk, grabbed his backpack, and closed it again.

"How's it goin', Danny?" Ricky said to me as I grabbed my own backpack from the back seat.

"Doin' all right. It's really fuckin' flat here, huh?"

"Fun fact: Illinois is actually the flattest state in the US," Ricky said.

"Which means good gas mileage," Ian said.

We walked inside Ricky's half of a one-story duplex and set down our bags. The place was small but tidy and posters of punk bands and volcanoes and maps lined the walls. A short, stocky man wearing a Metallica T-shirt under his long black hair was rolling a joint on the coffee table. He nodded to us as we passed through to the kitchen. "That's my roommate, Dave. He's in my program. Smart motherfucker." Ricky opened the fridge and grabbed some beers. We opened them and got to work.

The bathroom door was open.

"Nice place," I said. "What is it, two beds, one bath?"

"You're not gonna start getting weird again, are you, man?" Ian said.

"What are you talking about? I was just asking—"

"He's got this problem with the bathr—"

"What's that?" I pointed at a map where the world was upside down. I'd seen it a few times before and knew it had to do with rearranging people's perspectives on how they saw the world.

Ricky lit up. "That's a world map, but it's upside down. The whole point is to give people a different perspective on something they've become so accustomed to seeing. Did you even notice that?"

"Oh, no . . ." I said. I gulped my beer.

"I did," Ian said. "Any idiot could see that."

"You guys wanna blaze?" Ricky said.

"Fuck, I'll blaze," Ian said.

I nodded, and we returned to the living room just as the roommate, Dave, lit up the joint. He passed it around, and we caught a good buzz. Though fucked up, I couldn't stop looking at the bathroom. Maybe there was another in one of the bedrooms.

"You're a crazy motherfucker, Ian," Ricky said.

A good song came on the radio: "Roll with It" by Oasis.

"Damn, Mexico?" Dave said.

"Yeah, they got one of the world's most active volcanoes down there, and I'm gonna study it," Ian said.

Damn, this melody kicks right from the beginning. And those opening chords. . . . What the fuck were those. . . ?

"They're gonna kidnap your ass," Ricky said.

"Please, dude, I'm from Mexico. Nobody's gonna fuck with me."

Even though it's a pop song and the lyrics are trite as hell, it still somehow seems so alive and original. . . .

"I thought you were Greek or something?" Ricky said.

"Viva la Raza, whey," Ian said.

But, fuck, man, this radio's probably playing all nineties shit. . . .

Dave raised his hand in solidarity. "Viva la Raza!"

"Weren't you born in North Buffalo?" I said. God, shut the fuck up, man! Why'd you even say anything? After years of living with that other monster, don't you know better than to poke these fuckers with a stick?

"Yo, this dude tried to bring like six hundred pounds of gear with him. I show up at his house this morning, and he's carrying deep sea fishing poles and grizzly traps and shit. Who do you think you are? Davy Crockett or something?"

"All I had was a sleeping bag, tent, guitar—"

"And he was tryin' to play me songs he wrote the whole way through Ohio."

Dave and Ricky laughed.

"I swear, I'm gonna leave his Woody Guthrie ass on the side of the road somewhere."

"I'm paying half your gas."

"Christ, man, can't you just relax? You're killin' my buzz."

"There's a kegger tonight at some undergrad's house. You guys wanna go?" Ricky said.

"Fuck, I'm tired of all that frat bullshit," Ian said. "Let's just chill here and blaze."

"About that." Ricky became more serious. "My guy couldn't come through, so I don't have anything for you. But Dave here said he'd sell ya a few nugs."

Fuck! How are we gonna get all the way to the Pacific on just a few nugs? "That's cool," I said.

"Thanks, man. We'll figure something out," Ian said.

"Shit, after this morning, it's probably for the best," I said. "Plus, I'm not outrunning any grizzlies on weed-speed."

Dave and Ricky laughed again.

Ian didn't. "*Weed-speed*. Hey, *weed-speed*, guys. Hey, guys, I'm not gonna outrun any grizzlies on the *weed-speed*. You're such a fuckin' loser."

Dave and Ricky kept laughing.

I could feel the gripping getting worse: stomach, brain, ass. . . . Maybe it really was for the best not to get any more herb? With Dwayne's shit, I always caught a good high, but it was a gamble trying something new. I couldn't afford to experiment here. There was no place I could hide if shit turned bad. No bedroom to call my own. Each bathroom had like seven people waiting for it. The car wasn't mine.

The world outside belonged to the critical masses. I was as far out there now as I'd ever been, and there was no turning back. Some good herb could calm the nerves. Could get the creative mojo flowin'. But bad herb could be that final push over the edge into eternal darkness. I was living at the limit of sanity. Head so heavy I could barely move it. Mind so strangled up with horrific thoughts, it was ready to burn out. I had such difficulty speaking with people. Such difficulty looking in their eyes. Everything was the floor: gaze, spirit, soul. . . .

We smoked another J and got some food. Later that afternoon, Ricky, Dave, and Ian went to buy more beer and I stayed behind. I checked out the house. No one else was there. I looked outside. No one was around. I had to act fast. I started unbuckling my belt even before I got there, but then I thought of the Wiffle ball game Ricky kept saying he couldn't wait to play tomorrow and all the standing around and walking and partying. Fourth of fucking July. Just hold it in, man. It'll go away. You'll rip your ass to shreds.

I buckled back up, then went to the living room and pulled out my guitar. I tried to play something, but that something felt as if it were tearing me to shreds as well, so I put the guitar away and watched some tube. When the guys returned, we smoked some more grass. A few months back, I'd started noticing a sharp pain in my stomach anytime Ian was near. I couldn't open my mouth without him trying to shut it. Couldn't stand without him forcing me back down. I was stuck already. Stuck in the American Midwest. Stuck far away from any freighter that could take me off to new worlds. Far away from myself and any of the music I could feel raging through me.

It hadn't always been like this with him. At first, things were cool. At first, I'd never felt more inspired around someone. We'd get high and write songs, and we'd get drunk and rip on all the pretty-boy frat losers; we'd hit on girls and go streaking down Main Street. But the closer we got to graduation, the more I started to feel that pain in my stomach whenever he was around. We started doing things we'd only joked about before: breaking into houses just to prove we could; stealing cars and taking 'em for joyrides, then bringing them back without a scratch; ripping off small-time dealers—not even for the cash or drugs but to make them feel like the fools they were.

But now, I was the fool. Now, I was on an endless trip with a searing pain in my gut that wasn't going away anytime soon. And it was only getting worse. . . .

"You hear about Zach and Matt's band?" Ricky said.

"Yeah, man." Ian glanced at me. "They're blowin' the fuck up."

"Why didn't you guys keep playing with them? You fuckin' rocked," Ricky said.

Dave packed a bowl and ripped it.

"Well, they asked me like five times to play bass, but I wanted to drum, so I said no," Ian said. "Plus, I'm heading down to Mexico soon anyway."

Dave passed the bowl to the left.

"So, what are you guys studying again?" I said.

"But they didn't even ask his ass," Ian said.

"D-don't say that," I said.

Shit! "Man in the Box" came on the radio.

"Why didn't they ask you, Danny?" Ricky said. "You fuckin' rock on guitar."

You gotta get outta here! Go outside! Don't let that shit infect you. . . .

"Yo, Danny," Ian said. "He's talking to your ass."

"Oh, uh . . ."

"Shit, man, he's been like this for months," Ian said.

"What are you talking about?" I said. Fuck, that voice was already seeping into my subconscious. Get away before it takes over!

"It's like he's working on a five-second delay or something," Ian said.

"I was just thinking," I said.

"This is exactly how Paul Bern was acting before he lost it," Ian said.

"I heard that dude went nuts," Ricky said.

"D-don't talk about him!" I said. Layne's voice was getting louder inside my soul. Soon, it'd be all I could hear.

"He even looks like him, doesn't he?" Ian said.

"Yeah, a little," Ricky said. "They both got that boy-next-door thing going on. Well, maybe not with all that hair now."

"You better shave that shit before you start teaching this fall. Dude thinks he's Jim Morrison or something. They're gonna kick your burned-out ass right through the front door if you show up looking like that."

"Please . . . please don't talk about Paul," I said.

"Paul thinks he's on a spaceship or something," Ian said. "Even if he was here right now, he wouldn't know what the fuck we're saying."

I got up, walked to the bathroom, and locked myself in. Holy shit, I've been trapped my whole life, but I've never willingly walked into a trap like this before.

"He'll be in there for hours," Ian said, loud enough for me to hear. "But I shit faster than most people piss."

I tried to see myself in the mirror, but my vision was so blurred and thoughts so rapid I couldn't recognize anything outside of my own misery. I pulled out my flask and chugged as much cheap whiskey as I could.

Chapter 2

We woke up late the next morning to the smell of fireworks and hot dogs and phony patriotism. I'd slept on the floor and Ian the couch. Ricky was already up and trying to pump us up about the "Biggest fuckin' Wiffle ball game in Normal!" I ate a few pieces of white bread with butter, then headed outside into the beautiful, clear summer day. Ricky handed me a cup and pumped the keg, pouring me a beer. He and Dave had a huge yard, and Dave blasted Motörhead as we divided up into teams of eight—all guys from their geology program—and started the game. I was on Ricky and Ian's team, and Ricky was pitching like a major leaguer. Dude put some serious movement on the ball, and only a few of the guys from the other team were able to get on base. I got pretty fucked up, and after we crushed the other team, we ate some hot dogs and smoked some more grass. One of the guys started juggling flaming sticks while a few others shot off fireworks. It should have been a fun day, but I couldn't feel it. I mean, what the fuck were we even celebrating? Right then, we had troops going after "Al Qaeda" in Iraq. Right then, my buddy Sean was doing his second tour. Right then, the opioid epidemic on the East Coast was getting worse. Right then, a guy I grew up with who'd later OD was shooting up. Right then, my mother was getting screamed at by the bastard she'd never kick out. Right then, my depressed uncles were getting drunk as fuck and bitching about how they couldn't understand why my cousins were getting drunk as fuck and slipping away into nothingness. Right then, the music industry was dying, despite the best efforts of guys like Zach and Matt, who fucking ripped up any stage they went on. Right then, the poles were warming, and the terrorists were planning to bomb the fuck outta places like Mumbai, and Mexicans were scrambling over the border to reclaim the jobs they lost when NAFTA fucked up their farms. Right then, the pains in my stomach and ass were so unbearable I had no idea how to even think about the future. With such pain, every moment is about one thing and one thing only: escape. I felt as though all those phony-ass Middle America rockets were exploding inside my intestines. Inside my psyche. Inside my mind. I took a huge gulp.

"Yo, don't go too hard, man," Ian said. "You're driving tomorrow."

The next morning, we said goodbye to Ricky and Dave, who made good on his promise to sell us a few nugs, and took off much later than we'd wanted to. Dave's shit wasn't Da-Wayne, but it'd do. I drove us through Illinois and into Iowa. Something about all that flat land and being in the heart of America's breadbasket made me feel some slight patriotism. It was all so fucking foreign. I also loved the seventy-mile-per-hour speed limit and set the cruise control to ninety. Ian popped in some Depeche Mode but followed it with Maroon 5. He started singing along.

"Is this a joke?"

He was ready for me. "What do you mean, 'joke?' They keep rhythm way better than you ever could. And your fucking singing sounds like a dying yak."

"Fuck rhythm and smooth, clean sound. I'll take Crazy Horse to this shit any day. Fuck, I'd take a bunch of poorly trained monkeys playing Crazy Horse to this shit any day."

"You got the worst taste in music."

"I'm not the one playing Maroon fucking five. They represent all that's wrong with music today. Terrible lyrics, overproduced focus-group-driven sound, everything built for marketing and magazine covers, with pretty fucking singers with the most depressingly mediocre voices. They're a music-like substitute for people who can't handle real tunes."

"They're fuckin' jazzy, man. You would know it too if you weren't white trash."

"What'd you just call me?"

"Your whole fucking family's white trash. How many days a week you guys eat Burger King?"

"At least my dad's not in jail. What'd yours do again? Murder some dude?"

"Fuck you! I'll punch your ass right into oncoming traffic."

"Yeah, well, this car's going with me."

"I knew I shoulda brought Junkyard on this trip instead of you."

"Junkyard's so wacked out on meth right now, he probably thinks he's right there beside you."

"That's it. After Ames, you're walking home."

About a half hour passed before either of us spoke. Ian let the Maroon 5 CD play through a few songs—just long enough to flex his ego—then popped in some John Prine and quietly sang along to "Angel from Montgomery."

"Yo, can you do me a favor?" I said.

"Depends."

"Can you please not bring up any of that bathroom shit when we get there? I don't want Joanna to think I'm weird."

"Everybody already thinks you're weird."

"C'mon, man, I've been driving all day. I just want to relax."

"Fine."

"Let's smoke some of that herb."

Ian nodded, then pulled out the baggie and his bowl. We blazed through fields of corn, seeing the spinning gears of the America machine on our fucked-up quest for more, more, more. With a head full of weed, that beautiful scenery, and John Prine's voice guiding the way, I started to feel all right. Soon, we were in Ames.

I parked under a water tower with 'Ames, Iowa' written on it, and we walked up to a massive two-story house. Joanna was more Ian's friend than mine, so I let him knock. Joanna was another geology student, and she was a year into her grad program and already living in the house where she'd likely remain until it was time to dig her grave. She practically jumped on Ian when she answered.

"Oh my god, Ian! *Ahhhh!* You look so good."

I peered around her. Bathroom next to the kitchen and another by the door.

"Look at you, already living in a real adult house. What are you, like, forty-five now?"

"It's my parents' old house. They gave it to me when I graduated last year. C'mon, I'll show you around."

"You remember, Danny, right?" Ian said.

"Of course. Your hair's getting really long," she said.

"Yeah, it's been growing for about a year now," I said.

"I like it. You kinda got that Jim Morrison thing going."

Inside it looked like a typical Midwestern home: knick-knacks and picture frames and shit above the fireplace, doilies on the tables, one of those old-fashioned boxy wooden TVs. I was waiting for her to tell us her arm was tired from churning butter.

"So, how's the trip so far? You guys must be *sooo* excited!"

"Oh, it's, uh, been great," I said.

"Yeah, I'm just looking forward to getting out West," Ian said.

"Well, you're almost there. I think it's so cool that you guys are doing this. Not many people have what it takes for this kind of trip."

"Please, I've been all over," Ian said.

"Yeah, that trip we took down to Memphis was insane," she said.

"We definitely stayed in a crack motel," Ian said. "People were coming and going all night."

"Remember that crack pipe we found under the bed in my room?" she said.

"Yeah, it was sick," Ian said. "Yo, I heard you're gettin' married."

"Yeah, Richard finally proposed."

The house reeks of dust. . . .

"And he doesn't mind us staying here?" Ian said.

And mildew. . . .

"No. He's not going to be living here until after we get married. My parents were a little insistent on that."

The sink looks old as fuck. . . .

"And what about school?" Ian said.

A radio in the corner is playing "Cracklin' Rosie."

"I only have a few more years before I'm done. I can't wait to start my career. There are far too many people I graduated with who aren't doing shit right now. Just living at their parents' house and playing video games or doing drugs. But I'm making something of myself. I don't wanna be a loser."

God, that voice moves. . . .

"Look at you, all old and shit," Ian said.

"Don't knock it. I love curling up in my safe, warm house after a day of hard work. Life's slowed down, but it's still good. And I can't wait to get married. Richard is everything to me."

"I'm happy for you," Ian said.

"How about you? Got a girl yet?" she said.

And it's so powerful. . . .

"Nah, things didn't work out so well with Laura, and I'm not really feelin' dating anymore," Ian said. He smirked at me while saying to Joanna, "So, how's Delilah?"

Oh, you bastard.

"Yeah, how . . . how is she?" I said.

"She's good," Joanna said.

"I heard she's been fuckin' Brian Davis," Ian said.

"I think they just got together," Joanna said.

I hung my head.

"Come on," Joanna said. "I'll show you to your rooms."

We followed Joanna upstairs, and she showed us two rooms in the back. Ian claimed the bigger of the two, but I didn't care; mine had its own bathroom! We'd be leaving in a few days, so I only had to hold it in a bit longer. I dropped my bag in my room, but I got an uneasy feeling while checking out how clean and neat and homey it was. We went out for dinner, then headed to a bar near the university. The town was gorgeous, with much more character than I would have thought, given Iowa's reputation. There were trees and quaint shops all over. Safe little spot to hide away forever. The bar was packed with college kids, but we got a table in back near the jukebox and billiards tables. A group of paddle-asses near the bar were chanting as some kid chugged a glass of what was probably vodka. He looked ready to puke, and the pain on his face brought me back. It was a special kind of pain. A helpless pain. A hopeless pain. When I was in college, I'd usually go out five or six nights a week. Thursday, Friday, and Saturday were always celebrations. Everyone was dancing and singing and chugging beers and trying to fuck one another. But Sunday and Monday nights were different. The crowds had thinned, and you'd see the same faces over and over, and those faces always held that hopeless pain. There wasn't joy or celebration in what they were doing. I remember one guy in particular—some frat dude who was always out with a few other "brothers"—and he was always so drunk that it looked like his insides had ruptured and were starting to come up, and he was doing everything he could to keep from puking his chunky guts all over everyone. And his friends would buy him shots and dump whiskey in his beer when he wasn't looking and toss pills in his mouth and punch him in the dick and stomach and laugh. And he just took it all down with a look of excruciating pain. And these were his friends. These were guys he chose to spend his time with. On Thursday and Friday and Saturday nights, he'd still be there, but he got lost in the chaos. But it was clear to me on those Sunday and Monday and Tuesday nights that all college kids, just like everyone else, were out for blood—some just hid it better than others.

"So, you're *really* gonna study volcanology in Mexico?" Joanna said, pouring herself another beer from the pitcher.

"Yeah, why?"

"I dunno, because you never seemed to give a damn during undergrad."

"What are you talking about?"

"C'mon, really? You always showed up high—if you came at all—and all you did was clown around and try to make everyone laugh."

"Christ, man, I was just trying to lighten the mood. You fuckers can get so morbid sometimes."

"Nobody thought you'd finish. We just figured you'd end up doing something with music."

"I almost did. You remember my friend Doug Morricone? Came to visit a few times?"

"How could I forget that guy? He's famous now."

"He wanted me to play bass in his band, but I turned him down."

"Why?"

"Well, uh—"

I reached for the pitcher, but accidentally knocked it over. It spilled on the floor, but none got on anybody.

"What the fuck's wrong with you?" Ian said.

"Sorry, I was just trying to—"

"Yo, doesn't this dude remind you of Paul Bern?" Ian said.

"I heard Paul Bern went crazy," she said.

Paul Bern went crazy! Paul Bern went crazy!

"D-don't talk about him," I said. "Please."

"He looks just like him," Ian said. "They both got that, like, lunatic-next-door look, right?"

Some big drunk dude wearing an Iowa State T-shirt bumped into me while he was stumbling around.

"Watch it, fuckhead!" Ian shot to his feet.

"Wha—?" the drunk said.

"You just hit my friend," Ian said.

"Oh, sorry, man, I didn't mean to, uh, you know. . . ."

"Apologize." Ian got right in his face and looked ready to start swinging.

"He already did," I said.

"I'm s-sorry," the drunk said.

"Yeah you are, fucking fat drunk bitch. I should knock your ass out." Ian pressed his forehead into the guy's forehead and pushed him back.

"Stop, Ian!" Joanna said.

The guy staggered back a few steps with a look of fear in his eye. He was bigger than Ian—a lot bigger. But he had the fear. Ian didn't. Ian never did. The first night I hung out with him, he got into three separate fights. In one he challenged an entire frat house to take him on; no one did. He was a big fucker, but not the weight room kind. He wasn't rippling with muscle, but he had some serious strength and knew how to leverage his body to throw other people off balance. Though he never joined the wrestling team, he was friends with a lot of the guys on it, and he would regularly toss even the best of them around when they started messing with him. There was this deadness in Ian's eyes. This look that dared people to fuck with him. Most dudes were all talk. Shoving contests and insults. But Ian would cut somebody's ass and lick the blood off the knife. Something about that attracted me to him. Some realness inside of him most people didn't have. And I'd rather live in a real world full of anger and abuse than a fantasy world of rainbows and unicorns.

"Fuckin' little bitch," Ian said, as the guy returned to his group. They stared at us for a bit, but they were all pussies and just went back to drinking and ignoring the Ians of the world.

"He wasn't even starting shit with me," I said. "It was an accident."

"Nobody fucks with my friends."

"Just relax, Ian. God . . ." Joanna said.

We drank a few more pitchers, then staggered home. Ian was pretty fucked up, but I offered him some whiskey from my flask, and he took it down. We passed groups of college kids and some older whitebreads still in Iowa State gear. The scene looked to be getting to Ian. I knew it was getting to me.

"Look at these fuckin' fascists," he said to me.

"I try my best to ignore them," I said.

"You—you're not like these dudes. You're a good guy. You got a good heart. You shoulda just let me stomp that bitch back there, but you said not to. That's cool, man."

"I don't like seeing people get hurt, even if they deserve it."

"Yo, Delilah—you're better than Delilah too."

"Don't even talk about her—"

"She was a fucking cunt. You shoulda just opened your eyes and seen how bad she was jerkin' you around. She wasn't into you like you think she was."

"How the fuck could you know that? You didn't see the way she spoke to me. The way she touched me."

"You're way too naïve. That's why you're always getting hurt. You let everyone—especially chicks—walk all over you."

"I didn't let her walk all over me!"

"Come the fuck on, man."

"Hurry up, guys. I'm tired," Joanna said, walking on ahead.

I woke up the next morning on the front porch.

Fuck, fuck, fuck! What time is it? I checked my phone: eight thirty. When did Ian say we'd be leaving? Ten? Yeah, ten. Fuck! There's no time! I've missed my opportunity. FUCK! My stomach hurts so bad.

Just check though. Maybe you can still do it?

My right arm was asleep, so I opened the door with my left. It was quiet inside. I checked the downstairs rooms: no one. Upstairs, Joanna's door was open. She wasn't there, but Ian was sprawled in her bed.

Fuck! Should I do it? He could wake up at any moment—or she could come back. My stomach hurts so bad. Just do it. You gotta try. You'll be on the road all day.

I went to my room and quietly closed and locked the bedroom door, then started pulling off my clothes while hurrying to the bathroom. I closed and locked that door too, then sat on the toilet and instantly started pushing, even though I didn't have that feeling.

C'mon, man! Squeeze! You gotta do it *now*. There's no time to waste. I gripped a toilet paper roll and gave my guts everything I had. Tears started to fall from my eyes. You're disgusting! You're evil! This filth—this filth is the Devil. God is watching you. Delilah is watching. Matt and Zach and Doug and Ian—they're all watching. Your teachers and professors and parents and godparents. Everyone can see how disgusting you are. How ugly! How sinful! Hurry up! The car's leaving! Hurry! Everyone's getting married! Hurry! Everyone's buying houses and paying off their student loans and getting real jobs. And you're making filth. What girl could ever want you? You shoulda done this late last night while you had hours to relax. Now, squeeze! Push!

Holy shit! I feel it! Clamp down with everything you've got! All systems release. Don't worry about the pain. You'll be sitting for most of the day, anyway. Here it comes. I can feel it all passing, ripping open the wounds. God, how it hurts! Son of a bitch! *AHHHHH*! Hurry! Hurry! They're all coming! Was that the door? Is she back already? Push! Joanna's such a nice girl. How could you do this to her? In her house? She took you in, you ungrateful sack of shit! Squeeze! Squeeze with all your might!

Oh god, the pain is unbearable. I passed it all through, but the pain remains. The pain always remains. It ripped open my insides. I don't even want to wipe. It hurts too much. But you've gotta do it, man. Just grip that toilet paper roll. But don't scream. They'll hear you and come running. Come asking questions. Take your time with the wiping. Don't rip open any new wounds.

You know what? Fuck new wounds. The old ones weren't going anywhere, so why worry about the new? Add some new ones for all I care. Stick some needles up there too while you're at it. And wash it all down with hydrochloric acid. Bleach the fucker. Carve it out with a knife, then plunge that shit straight into your heart.

I first noticed the pain when I was about nineteen. I was working the maintenance crew at my neighborhood's town hall, and while shitting one day, it felt as if I'd just passed a razor blade. The pain stayed with me for a few hours but went away. But even after the pain had left, there was still itching and burning. Every other time I took a shit after that, it felt as if I was passing razors. The doctor told me I had an anal fissure, then handed me some creams. "It'll go away on its own in a few weeks." I used the creams, but it got worse. The doctor gave me more creams. "This should do the trick!" But the pain only intensified. Three years passed, and it'd gotten so bad, I didn't know how I could go on. It was always painful, but the pain was at its worst during those twenty-four hours after I'd taken a shit, so if I had an intramural basketball game or an important class presentation or something, I'd just hold it in. At first, it felt as if I was gonna explode, but after about an hour of squeezing and pulling all of my energy inward, the feeling would go away, and I could go three, four, five days—a week, even more— without shitting. But it was impossible to hold forever, and after I'd give in and go, it felt as if someone had just ass-fucked me with a bowie knife. It was excruciating to move, to sit, to lie down. It would bleed. It would leak. I knew I smelled. When the pain was at its worst, I'd only leave the house to go to class. The walk was torture, and when I got to the building, I'd head straight to the bathroom to wipe away the blood and shit while dripping tears and trying not to scream. It felt as if I had thumbtacks and glass shards up my ass, and as the whole world seemed to be marching ahead, I tried not to move. My grandfather'd had a colostomy bag, and this haunted my thoughts. It was already hard enough trying to make a connection with a woman, but with that bag between us it'd be impossible. The pain had gotten even worse since graduation, and the closer I came to my student teaching assignment in the fall, the more it felt as if I only had two ways out: music or death. This trip was literally everything for me.

Chapter 3

"We shoulda beat that dude's ass last night," Ian said as I drove us west down the I-80.

"It was an accident," I said.

"I fuckin' hate these clowns."

We cruised through endless flat green fields on a perfect clear blue day. It was hot as hell and the AC didn't work, so we kept the windows down. Sweat caked my body. I hadn't showered since the night before leaving Buffalo. It was too much of an ordeal, and the water just stung my ass anyways, so I figured I could put it off for a few more days.

The speed limit was seventy, and I pushed it to a hundred, roaring ever-closer to my dream of freedom in the West. I couldn't wait to see the Rockies, and I couldn't wait to get past them and roll down easy into California. The Promised Land. I knew I'd find an answer there. Knew the songs would leap from my chest like gazelles, hopping out into the world and spreading the real Good Word. Ian popped a mix of Mexican pop songs in the CD player and blasted the volume.

"I can't wait to get to Mexico." He grabbed an empty Nalgene and pissed in it, nearly filling it up.

"That's disgusting."

"What? I'll wash it before I drink out of it."

"I can stop."

"Fuck that."

The woman singing had the most gorgeous voice.

"I can't wait to get to Mexico either," I said.

"You brought your passport, right?"

"Yeah."

"You're gonna love it there. There's like, no rules. You can do whatever you want. There's a freedom there unlike any you'll ever find here. Forget all this Cali bullshit. Mexico is the true San Francisco."

"Well, I guess we're gonna find out."

"Yo, maybe we could play some tunes when we get to Nikki's."

"That'd be great! I feel some songs ready to burst out of me."

"She said there's gonna be a party tonight. We should save some of that green from Dave for tonight."

"I'm cool with that. Wanna toke a little now?"

"Sure."

Ian packed a bowl, and we blazed while cruising through one of the last remaining stretches of Real America. Farmers and plows and corn and blue skies. When the CD ended, Ian put in *American IV: Man Comes Around* and skipped ahead to "Personal Jesus." The endless green fields slowly turned into a series of rolling, golden-brown hills. Holy shit! Holy fuck! I made it! I made it to the West!

"Check it out, man!" I said.

"Yeah, it's intense."

Growing up in Buffalo, everything was snow white, or

summer green, or autumn orange, but I'd never seen Brown Earth. No trees, no corn—nothing but hills and sunshine and tumbleweeds blowing into the side of the car. It was the first time during the trip that I felt hopeful. That the spirit of the road was guiding and protecting me. That the Spirit of the Sixties was still alive and well and waiting to fill me with its infinite wisdom and inspiration as soon as I got *there*, man.

"Holy shit!" Ian stuck his head out the window.

"What?"

"Is that a tornado?"

I looked and sure enough, about fifty miles up the highway a tornado was blowing up a cloud of dust.

"This is incredible!" I said. I thought of the night I went to a friend's house in Plattsburgh with Paul Bern and a few other guys, and we got drunk and high as fuck, and I saw the Aurora Borealis for the first time while standing in a field beside the house. Then, that same night, I experienced my first earthquake—a 5.5 that shook the shit out of the house, knocking our empties off the tables and turning the tap water brown. The Aurora Borealis and an earthquake. Two wonderful examples of the beauty and power of nature that I'd experienced within five hours of one another. But here, it was more like five minutes. . . .

"You ever see a tornado before?" Ian said.

"No. I think the gods are trying to tell us something."

Ian cranked the volume, and I stepped on the gas, and we barreled toward that tornado as fast as we could. Not because we were thrill seekers out for a shot of adrenaline or because we wanted to take a scientific or artistic assessment of it or anything like that, but simply because it was in the way and we were moving forward through anything—and the bigger the obstacle, the faster we moved. Always forward. Never back. Retreat wasn't an option. If it sucked us right up to the heavens with it, we'd have gone with no fear.

When the song ended, Ian ejected the Cash disc, and Doug Morricone's voice was playing on the radio.

"Yo, Dougie is blowin' up, man!" Ian said.

"Christ, I wonder what he must think having his voice spread so far around the world."

"Oh god, I'm sure he loves it. That dude's always wanted to be a star. He used to climb up on my garage roof when we were like ten and pretend he was John Lennon on top of the Apple building, singin' 'Don't Let Me Down' an' shit."

Doug, Ian, and I grew up in the same neighborhood and went to high school together, but I didn't become friends with them until college. Ian and I both went to Conesus, but Doug skipped out on college and started a band that was now taking over the world.

We listened to the rest of the song, and when his voice faded out, I immediately thought of Paul Bern. Paul Bern never had a chance. He wrote songs too, and we'd play together sometimes. He was always looking for that extra spark to boost his creativity. He tried the natural path with yoga and hiking and all that jazz. But one night, Doug visited us at Conesus and sold Paul on acid: "This'll take you places you've never dreamed of going. It's what unlocked my creativity—I mean, I wrote my whole first album a week after dropping acid for the first time." Paul said, "Sure," and he and Doug dosed. Doug offered me some, but I declined, as did Ian. Instead, Ian talked me into doing shrooms with him. I'd never done them before, but Ian said they weren't much stronger than pot: "Just eat a stem. It'll give you a body high . . . Here take a cap too . . . Naw, you should take more. If not, you won't even feel it, so it's like a waste of good shrooms. . . ." So I took down more than half a baggie and he the rest of it, and the four of us went to a party. I remember standing beside a fireplace, feeling my spirit slowly flowing up the chimney and away. I knew if I just relaxed and let it take me, I'd wander away forever. So, I went outside and found myself again while looking at trees and leaves and grass. Even at night, the colors were so vivid. I think nature saved me. Paul wasn't so lucky. He dosed again over the next few weekends, and after only the fourth or fifth time, he went away and never came back. Soon we all started getting messages from him, warning us to protect our thoughts from aliens. Warning us that the intergalactic war was coming. Assuring us that he could speak to god, and that, if we followed Paul's word, everything would be all right. Most of the people he messaged were fucking spooked. Others made it into a joke. Paul was a brilliant songwriter. He was a math wiz, and he loved hiking through Letchworth. He could survive for weeks in the woods, living off the land. But now all anyone ever said about him was, "Paul Bern went nuts." You get cancer, and you're a hero. Get shot and they'll all gush over you. But you start hearing voices, and no one real will ever speak to you again.

Paul messaged me too, but I never responded. Nor did I visit him in the hospital. He was my fucking friend, and I left him hanging, just like everyone else. One night in particular, I was stoned and drunk and sitting by my computer, and he sent me an email begging me to respond. Fucking *begging* me. Everything got so dark and heavy, all

I could do was hit delete. It was then I realized for the first time, clear as fucking day: Nobody loves the insane.

"It looks like it's gaining strength," Ian said.

"So do we."

Later, the tornado died down and disappeared into the blue, and we got stuck in the hilly lull of northeastern Colorado.

"How much longer, you think?" I said.

"Just wait, man. It's incredible. You don't even see 'em coming—they just appear out of nowhere."

An hour later, they appeared. I'd been through the Appalachians and had lived in the Adirondacks, but nothing prepared me for the sheer power of the Rockies. They were on a different scale. These were *real* mountains—the kind people climbed and fell off of and died. That buried towns in boulders. That scraped the bottoms of planes.

"Yo, put that Cash disc back in, but play it from the beginning this time," I said. "And let it play through."

He popped the disc back in and blasted "The Man Comes Around." We'd played "Hurt" a few times with our band, and I think Ian wanted to avoid it, which is probably why he'd skipped over it last time.

"Have you heard from Zach and Matt at all?" I said.

"Yeah, I spoke with Zach a few weeks ago, and he said they're blowing up too. They're opening for Jakob Dylan at Lafayette Fest next month."

"Oh, that's, uh, good for them."

Ian and I became friends in our junior year. I ran into him at a bar one night, and we went back to his place to toke and play some music. We started getting together a lot more after that and spent most of that time getting high and writing tunes. I was good at starting melodies and he was good at finishing them, as well as coming up with bridges that kicked. In the start of our senior year, Ian asked me to play rhythm guitar for the band he'd put together with Zach and Matt. The two had been in the biggest band on campus since we were freshmen, but they'd broken up the summer before our senior year. I'd never been in a band before and was nervous to play with such talented musicians. But right from the first practice, everything clicked. We'd usually meet at Ian's place, get high, and jam in the living room. We started playing covers—Van Morrison, the Band, the Dead, Talking Heads, Robert Palmer—but our own stuff seeped into the mix. There was some feeling I got playing in that living room that was unlike anything I'd ever experienced. I'd just be standing there, facing the corner of the room, but with a guitar in my hands, playing along with such talented guys, I was at the center of everything, rising up and ascending to the heavens. Even though their skills were leaps and bounds ahead of mine, I felt right in step with them, plugged into their spirits and able to elevate the songs above the chords and lyrics to something divine.

In that living room, I felt immortal. I was free to experiment. Free to express myself. Free to connect. I felt us working together. Felt as if I was finally doing what I was meant to. Felt as if I wasn't alone.

But playing at bars or parties with fifty-plus people watching was a different experience. I became rigid and closed off and felt completely isolated. I tried not to look into the crowds: chugging and screaming and blood rushing to their loins. The music seemed to be nothing more than a sideshow to them. So I held on tightly to the songs to survive the chaos. I gripped my guitar and kept my eyes on the floor. The songs were like turds I had to squeeze out of me. I'd fuck up chords, miss lyrics, slaughter solos. But still the people cheered. Soon, *we* became the biggest band on campus. I knew Ian felt it too. He started making excuses not to practice and he'd show up late to shows. I could hear Matt and Zach moving a thousand miles ahead. I could feel them pulling out ahead of me, and my hands and head just couldn't keep up. My heart was right there with them. My soul was further out than any of us could go. But my hands were stone. I started getting horrible anxiety attacks before shows, and instead of warming up, I'd drink as much as I could just to get through. And when we'd start playing, sometimes I'd just stop and look around. No one seemed to notice. No one seemed to care. Just more applause. No matter what I did, they'd cheer. I'd been on pace to graduate summa cum laude, but I pretty much stopped attending class that second semester, and my GPA dropped like a rock. But still we got bigger. Everyone seemed to know me. Everyone said hi. People who'd never spoken to me before. People who'd once called me weird. Girls who'd only given me dirty looks. Frat assholes who'd beaten the shit out of my friends. Sometimes I'd look into the crowd and see them. I hated them. And I started to hate music.

Ian and I went to a bar one night about a month before graduation and saw Zach and Matt playing with a new bassist and rhythm guitarist. It was worse than any breakup. We hadn't made love, man—we'd made *music* together. I'd already been going hard that last year and a half, but that last month was a total haze. I probably would have ended up in the hospital a few times, but college kids don't bring people to the hospital, so I came through on my own. I'd taken some bad spills but no one seemed to care. It seemed the drunker I got, the louder they all cheered. And as the world around me was blossoming, I was withering away. I had no more shows left—just the road. Ian and I started breaking into places and stealing cars and fucking with people and getting in fights, and soon we turned on one another. I hated being young. I hated being sad. The world hates the young and sad, and it should. But as long as I was on that road, I was never gonna grow old.

We reached Denver just as the sun was starting to drop behind the Rockies, and we continued through the city and up into the mountains. We stopped at a small gas station beside a gorgeous green cliff. The air was pure and crisp and the energy youthful and vibrant. We walked to the edge of the road, and I handed my camera to a young backpacker Ian had started talking to. He snapped a shot of us standing above a huge drop-off into a green valley. "You guys must be having a hell of a time! I wish I could join you." We hopped back in the car and continued up the winding mountain roads and soon arrived in the small town of Ski Park. Ian gave me directions, and I parked in front of an apartment complex behind a supermarket.

"Ian!" Nikki ran out and hugged him. "Holy shit, you made it!"

Ian looked uneasy, but he always looked uneasy when hugging people. "Yeah, we made great time. This dude's got a lead foot."

"It was such a beautiful drive," I said.

"Man, you guys must be tired," Nikki said.

"Naw, I'm ready to party," I said.

"Good, because there's a huge party at a cabin in the woods starting in a few hours. I wasn't sure if you'd wanna go."

"Yeah, let's do it," Ian said. "But let's get some food first."

"I got some leftover pizza in the kitchen," Nikki said.

"Is it—?" Ian said.

"Don't worry, it's veggie."

"Cool."

We followed Nikki inside her apartment, which she shared with one of the managers of the ski resort where they both worked. The manager's name was Katie, and she was thirty-five and looked burned-out as hell. Her smile had no life behind it. Nikki had two couches and said we could each take one. Ian called the bigger one, but I didn't care. I was getting drunk as fuck and didn't give a shit where I slept. We devoured the rest of the pizza, then hopped back in the car and headed through town.

"In the winter, this place is packed with skiers, but right now, there are probably only about a thousand people here and most work at the resort," Nikki said.

"What do you do out here for fun?" Ian said.

"You're about to find out," she said.

Nikki drove us higher up into the mountains, and I could hear the celebration long before we arrived at the three-story cabin in a heavier section of forest. Nikki parked, and we followed her inside.

An explosion of energy. There had to have been forty or so people packed into the living room and kitchen, chugging, smoking, dancing, chanting—one guy was even giving tattoos in the corner. We went through the kitchen and onto the back porch where about twelve people were sitting in plastic chairs and pounding beers. Nikki introduced us to the main crew: Tania was a small, energetic hippy chick a little older than us. She was cute, but I already knew she wouldn't be into me. Even though I looked the part, I could tell instantly she was way more hardcore than I was. Teddy and Kyle were a few years younger and looked as if they'd just gotten back from Warped Tour: punk band T-shirts, tattoos, ear gauges, piercings. . . . They were ripping a huge bong, and they let me and Ian hop in on the rotation. Lance was a mountain man from Arkansas. He was burly and bearded and wore a thin flannel button-down and spoke about how much he loved nature. They all lived in the house and worked at the resort, and they threw parties almost every night.

"We get great drugs up here, but they're few and far between," Tania said.

"Yeah, we gotta wait for the shipments to come in from Denver, but it's always worth it," Teddy said.

"What do you get?" Ian said.

"Anything you want: pills, heroin, crack, meth, coke, weed . . ." Tania said.

"Yeah, we just scored some great crystal," Lance said. "You guys down to smoke?"

"Oh, no thanks," I said. "I just stick to weed."

"We got some great opium too," Teddy said. "Shit'll mellow you right out."

Ian got up to grab a beer, but took one step, shook his head, and dropped back down.

"Take it easy, man," Lance said. "You're almost ten thousand feet up right now."

"Yeah," Tania said. "You guys should go easy on the beers for a few days until you get used to it."

"And drink a lot of water," Kyle said.

"And smoke some crack, muthafuckas!" Teddy said.

We drank a shitload of beer, then Nikki, Ian, and I drove up to the highest peak in the area. I passed around my flask, and we killed it by the time we parked the car. The stars were brighter than I'd ever seen, and I felt as if I could lick them. I ripped off my clothes and jumped into a snow bank. Ian did the same, and we ran around screaming off the top of the US.

Ian stopped screaming and stared at the shimmering lights of the world below.

"The West," he said.

"What?" I said.

"We're on the Continental Divide right now. That down there's the West."

I stared as well, then stepped forward and took a piss. Ian laughed.

We came to a bridge with a sign on it warning us not to cross.

"Yo, I bet you won't do it," Ian said to Nikki.

"Of course I won't," Nikki said. "I'm not a fucking idiot."

"I am," I said. I stepped onto the bridge. It felt solid, but what the hell did I know?

"Cross to the other side and come back," Ian said.

"K." I headed deeper into the dark. I could hear creaking and felt the bridge start to sway.

"Keep going!" Ian shouted.

Suddenly I was back onstage at our last show—at least, *my* last show. We were playing at one of the biggest frats on campus—a frat notorious for beating the shit out of anyone who so much as looked at them wrong. They'd fucked up a bunch of my friends, and I felt sick having to play there. That afternoon, I got as drunk as I could before Matt drove us and all our gear over in his station wagon. We were playing outside on their huge back porch, and while it had been sixty degrees that afternoon, it'd dropped down into the thirties while we were setting up, so I'd put on some thick gloves to keep my hands warm. As usual, Ian showed up just before we started playing. I took off the gloves, but my hands instantly turned to stone, and I knew the night was fucked. I'd found some yellow-tinted ski goggles in the back of Matt's station wagon earlier that day and wore those instead. When it was time, I started on the opening of the Dead's version of "Turn On Your Love Light." I kept waiting for the others to jump in, but they were passing a joint, so I continued alone. At first, I kept my eyes on my guitar, but then I made the mistake of looking into the crowd and fucked up one of the notes. But everyone went wild. The other guys kicked in, and I purposely fucked up a few notes and everyone went nuts again. I looked into the crowd: there had to have been four or five hundred people chanting and chugging and dancing like maniacs around flaming oil barrels and offering up human sacrifices. With the yellow tint from the goggles, it all looked like some fucked-up scene from *Apocalypse Now*. I stopped playing and spoke into the mic: "There's blood in the water!" And they all cheered. "You don't know what you're doing!" And the band kept going. I got off the porch and started walking through the crowd. Some guys tried to slap me up and some girls grabbed my arms and ass, but I ignored them and kept moving. I started grabbing drinks out of the frat brothers' hands, chugging them, and tossing the plastic cups in their faces, and they all went wild. When

Ian and the other guys took a break, Ian and I went inside the house and started pissing all over the couch while about a dozen of the brothers cheered us on. Then we grabbed a few chairs and some of their frat jackets and shit, brought 'em outside, and started burning them in the flaming barrels. Still the frat assholes cheered like animals. We got back on the porch and started playing again, but I was over it—I was over music and people and. . . .

At the end of the show, one of the brothers gave Matt a hundred bucks, and we walked to a nearby bar and blew it all on shots. After, Ian and I started walking home, but Ian gave me this look and said, "Follow me," and though I didn't know the details, I knew what he wanted to do. The frat house was halfway down a steep grassy hill and just above the highway. We walked to a car parked on a street above the house, and Ian started looking around. "You see a rock or brick or something?" I glanced around, then checked the handle. The door opened. Ian got in the driver's seat and I the passenger seat, and he hotwired the car and drove it until we were above the garage. He turned onto the grass, put it in neutral, and jumped out right as the car started rolling forward. I, however, shifted over into the driver's seat.

"Yo, hop out, man!" Ian shouted.

"No," I said to myself. The car picked up speed and headed straight for the garage.

"HOP OUT, DANNY!"

Closer and closer.

"YOU'RE FUCKING CRAZY!"

At the last moment, I jerked the wheel hard to the right, missing the garage. I jumped out and rolled beside the back fence where there were still about a hundred people partying on the other side. When I got up, they all went wild. I knew it right then, that they, like all the others, were cheering for my death.

Our death. . . ?

"YO, WHERE THE FUCK ARE YOU?" Ian screamed as he ran down the hill.

The car kept rolling across the highway and down into the valley. It kept rolling, rolling, rolling right into the dark void. Out of memory. Out of existence. Rolling forever into oblivion.

"C'mon, man, keep going!" Ian said again.

I stopped, turned around, and walked back toward him and Nikki.

"You're a little bitch," he said as I hopped off the bridge.

"And you're just like all the others," I said. "You fucking changed, man."

I woke up the next morning in the backseat of the car with the worst hangover I'd ever had, likely because of the altitude. But at least I was fully dressed. I walked into the apartment, where Nikki and Ian were drinking Bloody Marys. They handed me one, and I took it down with a quickness.

Ian and I were running low on supplies, so we walked down to the supermarket, split up, and got what we needed. I put my groceries inside the small cooler I'd also bought, along with a bag of ice, and carried it outside, but when Ian saw it, he lost his shit.

"Fuck that, you gotta take it back!"

"Why?"

"It'll weigh down the car!"

"It's the smallest one they had."

"I don't give a shit, take it back!"

"C'mon, man, I just bought all this bologna and yogurt—"

"Bologna? You're fuckin' sick, you know that?"

"It'll go bad!"

"Fine, you can keep the cooler, but you can't fill it with any ice."

"What the fuck's the point of that?"

"Ice is too heavy."

"You gotta be kidding me."

"Ditch the ice, or I'll leave your ass up on a mountain somewhere all alone. . . ."

I tossed the ice in nearby garbage can.

That afternoon, we met up with the cabin crew and went Frisbee golfing, or frolfing, at a gorgeous course a few miles away, with mountains and evergreens forever in the distance. We got hammered and smoked some great bud, then headed back to their place for another party. When we got to the house, there were already several other people inside, smoking the gravity bong in the living room and doing shots in the kitchen. Some waved and said hello as the home's actual residents walked in, but most just continued getting fucked up. I spent most of the night pounding beers, smoking joints, and watching episodes of *The Andy Milonakis Show* with some dudes from Kentucky working at the ski resort for the year. They gave me some pills and opium, "For the right occasion, man," and I said thanks, then got up to use the bathroom. I passed a small room where Nikki, Tania, and a few others were smoking meth. I walked past the bathroom and continued outside, as far from that sweet, shower-curtain smell as possible, and pissed off the back deck. There were a couple of dudes passed out in the plastic chairs. Ian was behind them, talking with some cute girl. I listened to their conversation.

"Holy shit! You know Doug Morricone?"

"Please, he's one of my best friends. He used to sleep over at my house all the time. He asked me to play bass in his band, but I said no."

"Why?"

"I'm heading down to Mexico to work on the world's most active volcano."

"Oh my god, that's *so* cool!" But soon someone came out asking if anyone wanted to do a keg stand, and she said yes and disappeared back into the house.

Ian came over. "Yo, I'm gettin' the fuck outta here." He looked at the passed-out dudes.

"I think Nikki's too fucked up to drive us back."

"I'm just gonna run back."

"It's like six miles."

"That's nothing, man. I can do thirteen no problem."

"We're up in the woods. Aren't there like bears and wolves and shit?"

He took a look around, then grabbed a hatchet leaning against the house. "I'm good."

"How the fuck am *I* supposed to get back?"

"How the fuck is that *my* problem?"

"This is fucked up."

"This party's fucked up. I'm sick of talking to these burnouts. I'm dippin'. Peace."

He walked down the steps and disappeared into the darkness. I looked at the passed-out dudes, then at the house. I turned, leaned forward against the deck's rail, and stared into the void.

I woke up the next morning feeling like shit. When I opened my eyes, it took me a minute to realize I wasn't at the cabin but on a couch in an unfamiliar living room. I could hear at least two guys talking in another room.

"Yeah, I got some welding jobs later today, but I might cancel."

"All right, all right, cool, man, cool."

Judging by how high up we looked to be and how the front door was just across the living room, I figured this was an apartment. Soon, the guys came over. The welder was a big dude: tall, rugged, built like a Marine. He wore a stained white T-shirt and worn jeans. The other was a thin, weasel-looking dude, who spoke much quicker than normal.

"Mornin'," the welder said to me. "You want coffee or something?"

"No, but thanks. Where the hell am I?"

"Don't remember, do you?" the welder said.

"Not at all."

"We came back here after the party to smoke some grass," the weasel dude said. "Kenny here's got some great shit."

"We were just about to toke. Care to join?" the welder said.

"Yeah, sure."

The weasel packed a bong while the welder put on *Magical Mystery Tour*. We passed the bong and shut the fuck up and listened to the music. Right from the title song I felt as if I was in this strange yet familiar and safe place. It was one of those special moments: strangers plugged in together, sharing an almost spiritual experience in some shitty apartment on the roof of America—an America with eggs and bacon and OJ in its sleepy eyes—and I was hungry too but kept ripping that bong with the gentle welder and emaciated weasel and the CD played on. But by "Penny Lane," the weasel pulled out a bag of junk and a syringe, cooked up, and mainlined it.

"Want somma this?" he said to us.

"Sure," the welder said.

"Uh . . ." I said.

The weasel cooked up another shot and passed it to the welder just as "All You Need Is Love" came on. The welder, however, gave it to me. "Guests first." When I was a kid and the Evil Thoughts would come on, sometimes I'd pop in my dad's Beatles *Anthology 1*, and replay "Besame Mucho" and "The Sheik of Araby" over and over until the melodies got stuck in my head and drowned out the Darkness. And it was John Lennon's voice that saved me that morning. Here I was in this stranger's apartment, on his couch, smoking his weed, listening to his music. He was much bigger than I was. I didn't know what he was capable of. From all my previous experience, I knew to just say yes so as not to poke the beast. The dark energy was flowing against the current right up my veins toward my heart and soul. Everything was against me. I was so tired—so fucking tired. Tired didn't even come close. It was an exhaustion so deep and heavy it ached. So deep down in my cells and DNA, I stood no chance. But it was John Lennon's voice that gave me the push to say, "No, thanks." Perhaps they'd cut me down. Perhaps they'd kick my ass. Perhaps they'd kill me.

But the welder just said, "Cool," and banged it himself. John Lennon, my Savior! My Sweet Lord! He filled me with all I really needed. And Praise Be to the Welder! Who could have crushed me with his hands! Praise Be to Kindness! I was at the world's mercy, and the world was not often kind. When *Magical Mystery Tour* ended, the welder played *Let It Be* and skipped ahead to "Across the Universe." He leaned back, closed his eyes, and said, "This is my favorite song, man. It heals me."

When the song ended, I took off without saying goodbye, and even though I had no idea where I was, I looked to the mountains, oriented myself, and found my way back to Nikki's apartment, replaying "Across the Universe" in my head the whole way. They were up and drinking already. Drinking already. Drinking already. Paul Bern liked to drink in the mornings. Paul Bern was already drinking. Drinking already. Already drinking. . . .

Chapter 4

We'd planned to leave for Yellowstone that afternoon, but Nikki talked us into staying another night. "C'mon, the guys are throwing a huge party tonight. It's gonna be great." We ate some PB&J sandwiches, smoked some grass, and headed to a saloon. We sat with a few of Nikki's friends at a wooden table near the big window in front. Ian only lasted about forty-five minutes before he ran back to the apartment, but Nikki and I stayed. One friend, a cute brunette, got closer and closer to me after each drink. She started running her fingers through my hair.

"It's so soft. What do you put in it?" she said.

"Air."

She laughed. "I think it's so cool you're gonna be a teacher. How old are you?"

"Twenty-two."

"It's so great that you've already got your shit together. I'm twenty-six, and I never even went to college—just started working at the resort. I have no idea what I want to do with my life, but clearly you do."

I got up to use the bathroom, but the bartender kicked me out after seeing me take a nip of whiskey from my flask as I walked over. I knocked on the window, and Nikki said goodbye to the others. We went to another bar and got loaded, then went to the party, and I woke up the next morning in the hallway of the wrong floor of Nikki's apartment complex. Some older woman hissed at me as if I were a stray cat she was trying to shoo away. I found Nikki's apartment, and again she convinced us to "just stay one more night, please?"

The three of us met up with the cabin crew at a pub. We sat at the bar, drinking cheap beers, and decided to order food. When I asked for a hot dog, Ian started laughing.

"A hot dog? Can you believe this guy?" Ian said. No one even looked at him, but still, he went on. "Hey, Danny, remember that time you ordered a hot dog at a gas station in Louisiana? Yo, check it out, guys—this dude eats station dogs!"

A few of them ordered hot dogs too.

"And remember that time I had to drive you to the hospital because you had that lump on your nut?" Ian said.

I left the bar and went to sit in the passenger seat of Ian's car. I'd driven us there and still had the keys, so I started the car and popped a random CD in the player—Ian's Mexican pop mix. That beautiful voice came back through the speakers. Christ, I had no idea what she was saying, but the melody and the power and feeling of her voice—I knew, just knew, she felt every emotion she was singing about. I couldn't help but break into tears. Please, I know I don't know you, but I can tell you get it. I know you understand. Please, if I don't make it, tell them I was good. Please, tell them I was clean. Please, tell them I went down fighting. Write them a song about me. Make me happy. Make me strong. I've been trying so hard to write this song myself, but I can't do it. There's something wrong with me. I can feel the emotion inside. I can feel the beauty. Feel the art. But for whatever reason, it overwhelms me, and I just can't see it long enough to paint it. Can't hold it still long enough to understand it. To give it proper release. Please, give them something powerful. Make them feel special and safe. Make them feel loved. I've loved them all so much, even though they've hurt me so badly. Even though they've tried to kill me so many, many times while laughing and pointing their fingers. Why do they laugh? I still love them. I still want them to know how special they are. Even if it kills me. I wish they could see what I see. That even when I spat at them and clawed at their eyes, I did it because I couldn't deal with how badly they hurt us. With how obstinately they'd rejected my pleas for us to try to understand ourselves and find a way to feel better. I just wanted to know them. To love them. Please, tell them my body was clean. That it wasn't broken or in such excruciating pain. Please tell them I wasn't insane. That I never had such dark thoughts. Please, tell them so I don't just disappear. And please, bring back Paul Bern. He's just a kid. He was just experimenting. He didn't deserve to lose it all. Please. I feel your song inside of me. I know it's there, but I'll never be allowed to sing it. The journey to it is too long and dangerous. I see that now. Please. He'll be back soon, and we won't be able to talk again. Please, I'm twenty-two, and I'm so sad it hurts.

The collar of my shirt was drenched. My stomach and ass were stinging. I couldn't go on. There was no way.

But that voice. . . . I knew there was something in it. Some force that belonged just as much to me as it did to her. Something in that voice was calling me. "Come to Mexico. The secret is here. Here, you'll find what you need. Come. Your family is waiting for you. Your life is waiting for you." I trusted that voice more than I'd trusted the voice of god. The voice of the priests. Of the teachers or presidents or grandparents or parents. I trusted that voice. I trusted that voice. But was it just a trick? Were the Dark Thoughts fucking with me? Had they disguised themselves?

When the song finished, I let the next one play, but it didn't give me the same feeling as the first. I shut off the car, wiped away my tears with my shirt, and went over to a spigot and started washing my face just as Ian came outside.

"What the fuck are you doing?" he said.

"J-just washing my face."

"I think that's the closest to a shower you've come in a week. Everybody's been talking about how bad you stink."

"So do you. When was the last time *you* showered? Not since we left Buffalo."

"They're dragging us to another party soon. We should get the fuck outta here, man. I can't take this shit anymore."

"Naw, let's stay a few more days. I wanna go to the costume party tomorrow night."

"None of these chicks are gonna fuck you smelling the way you do."

"I don't smell that bad."

"You smell like a tweaker's asscrack."

Later, we went to a different house with a ton of land and horses and got drunk while watching surfing videos on TV. California, I need you. You don't know how fucking badly I need you. You better deliver. . . .

The next morning, I woke up on the floor beside an

empty bed in the party house. I felt tremendous pressure in my gut, but I couldn't do it yet. Tonight was the costume party! Maybe I'd meet a real girl. A cute girl. One with a golden voice and a heart of dynamite. I needed to be in top shape. I went to the bathroom and washed my face, pits, and crotch, then headed to the living room where Ian and Nikki were sleeping on separate couches. Christ, the house was gorgeous: high ceilings with exposed wooden beams overlooking a sweeping mountain valley. When Ian and Nikki woke up, we smoked a bowl with the guy whose parents owned the house, then headed to town for lunch.

After, Ian drove us back to Nikki's place and demanded that I pack my stuff and put it in his car, "So we can leave as early as possible in the morning." I should have known, but I was stoned and went along with it. Nikki went over early to help set up for the party, and Ian and I watched *La Bamba* until it was time. We piled into Ian's car and took off, but he went the wrong way down the main road.

"They should have plenty of drinks there," I said. "No need to bring anything."

He didn't respond, just kept driving. About fifteen minutes later, he pulled over in a parking lot beside what looked like an abandoned liquor store and shut off the car.

"What the fuck's going on?"

"We're sleeping here tonight so we can get an early start tomorrow."

"Are you fucking kidding me? What about the party?"

"Fuck the party. I'm sick of those losers."

"Those losers have been cool to us all week. A lot cooler than you."

"You wanna go so badly, then go."

"Maybe I will!"

"But if you do, I'm leavin' your ass up in the mountains with all the fucking bears and burnouts."

"You got something seriously wrong with you!"

"Fuck you, Paul Bern! At least people don't talk about how weird I am behind my back."

"No, they talk about how sadistic you are."

"Say another word, and I'll knock you out and drag you into the highway." His dead eyes teemed with dark energy.

"Fuck it."

He closed his eyes and fell asleep. I tried to do the same but felt such a searing pain in my stomach, I thought it'd eat right through me. I pulled out my flask, but it only had a few shots left. FUCK! What am I gonna do? Wait, there's a liquor store right there. But it looks closed.

I got out of the car and shut the door quietly so as not to piss off Ian. The store was dark outside and in. I tried the front door but it was locked. I walked around back, but that was locked too. Ian could've picked the lock, but no way was I waking that maniac up. Look for a rock or something. But what about the alarm? Fuck it, I need to get in there! I looked down the road. Nothing for miles in either direction. Just try it, man. Maybe there's no alarm. You grab a few bottles and leave some cash, and it'll all be okay. In fact, you'll be doing the owner a favor, giving them business outside of normal hours. The glass in the back door is cracked anyways. This'll give them reason to replace it.

I walked around the lot searching for a rock big enough to do the job, but when I pressed my face against the front window, I realized the store was completely empty—I couldn't see a single bottle.

Maybe Ian's got some beer in the trunk? I went back to the car, but the keys weren't in the ignition. He must've had them. Fuck this! Seriously, fuck this! My fucking stomach was killing me. I grabbed my cooler out of the backseat and put it beside the car, then sat on it and leaned against the passenger door. The chemicals were racing and my muscles were squeezing the worst they had in months. Oh god, how could you let yourself get into this situation? This is crazy. This is fucking crazy. You know you should get away from this dude, but you won't. I know you won't. You've got yourself convinced you're strong—honorable, even—for putting up with this abuse, but it's all bullshit. And you know it. But you won't do shit about it because you're weak. You're pathetic. Anyone else would have run by now. But not you. You're not like the others. They're strong and you're weak. They're good and you're bad. They're smart and you're stupid. You're so ugly. You smell so fucking terrible. Just do it, man. Just do it now. End all the bullshit. There's a hatchet in the back seat. Just a few whacks, and it'll all be over. The whole fucking nightmare, done. So simple. Just lean back and go to sleep forever.

But I need this trip, and I can put up with so much more than anyone else. That has to mean something, right? And because of that, maybe I'll find something on these roads that no one else would be able to find. Something that will save us all. I pulled out my flask and killed it, then remembered the pills and opium the guys from Kentucky had given me. I popped a few pills, but I had just enough resin in my bowl to get a decent high, so I saved the opium for later. I woke up the next morning with my back against the car door. A semi passed by and might as well have been in my head.

"Let's get the fuck outta here." Ian grabbed something from the trunk and slammed it shut. "But you're driving." He tossed me the keys.

Chapter 5

ore Morrissey—*You Are the Quarry*—as I blazed up the 125 and into Wyoming. Though the mountains dried out into dusty humps, the scenery here was just as beautiful as any other spot we'd yet seen, and it filled me with just as much wonder. The second we crossed the state line, I pushed the Camry up to about one thirty. The road was empty and the day gorgeous, so conditions seemed perfect for pushing life to the max. It was about a hundred degrees outside, and even with the breeze we were sweating our asses off. I could feel the crud layering on my skin and knew I'd need to shower soon. You could only push this so far before the rot would begin eating you away. I'd been gunning it for about half an hour before a car appeared on the horizon and sped toward us. By the time I realized it was a cop car, it was too late to slow down, so I just kept pushing it. But the cop just pointed at me as if to say, "Slow the fuck down, heathen!" and kept driving. Maybe there was some Wild left in the West after all. Regardless, I dropped down to about a hundred and continued pushing up the 287, then the 26, until we hit Grand Teton National Park. Holy shit was it gorgeous! The slides my geography professor showed us at Conesus were nothing compared to that sparkling sunlight dancing on top of the Snake River as it flowed below those snow-capped peaks. We parked and took some pictures, and Ian was actually pretty cool when I asked him to take a shot of me in front of the sign welcoming us to the park.

I couldn't wait to get into nature—to get away from the crowds and the filth and the judging eyes. I'd be able to strip down to nothing and cleanse myself in the freshness of earth.

We hopped back in the car and continued to Yellowstone. The traffic got heavier the closer we got to the park. A moose grazed in a field to our left, and the driver of an SUV heading in the opposite direction pulled over so quickly, he almost flipped it. The woman sitting in the passenger seat looked to be yelling at him, and he buried his face in his hands. A skunk ran into the road, and I crushed it. I had enough time to swerve, to swerve, to swerve, but I didn't. I wasn't sure why, and this tormented me. I started getting a sick feeling the closer we got to the park's entrance, and it got worse when we finally arrived at our crowded campsite. Fuck! I knew there'd be other people around, but this was ridiculous; the tents were so close it looked as if we'd all be together in one big group. There were a few public bathrooms beside some bear-proof garbage cans, and a lone buffalo wandered around the scene. Some people inched closer and closer to it, despite signs everywhere showing pictures of buffalos goring motherfuckers. I hoped it'd get pissed and start going apeshit on all these foolianis, but that'd be a shitty way to start our adventure here. We found our spot and set up Ian's tent. I figured now was the time to use the bathroom. I was so distracted with the stress from the drive and the beauty of the park that I figured I could fool myself into letting one slip out before my mind even knew I was doing something bad. I told myself I was just going to piss, but I went into a stall and started pulling down my pants. I started getting the feeling, but a woman outside was laughing the most piercing, arrhythmic laugh, and that was it for me. I finished pissing, pulled up my pants, and went back to the tent. I was surprised to see Ian sitting on top of our picnic table, playing guitar.

"We should jam later," he said.

"That'd be great."

I felt like writing a song, but it was so fucking loud: fat, loud, white Americans being fat, loud, white Americans while grilling, using the bathroom, throwing out their trash, setting up tents. . . . Everything was hilarious. Everything needed to be said several volumes too loud. Every fucking squirrel that passed needed to be photographed. Kids screaming. Parents screaming. Fuck this. . . .

I'd brought earplugs with me but knew not to put them in. Put 'em in once and you'll never stop using them. The skin in your ears used to open and flake out when you were a kid. Just keep them in your pocket—save them for an emergency.

This wasn't what I'd had in mind when I'd thought of the West. I wanted bright green fields, crystal mountain streams, clean air, sunny skies. . . . I wanted to lie in a bed of soft grass and listen to the wind blowing through the trees. Hear the rain and concentrate on all the sounds it made. Listen to the birds and other animals telling me their stories.

We could have gone backcountry camping, but we didn't have the first idea what we were doing, and there were bears and wolves and thick mazes of forests out there. Christ, being alone took such skill and put you so close to real danger. I guess the fucking tent-ement was where I belonged. . . .

Ian and I grilled some soy dogs, played some music, and went to sleep. His tent was built for two people, but it was really meant for one. We squeezed in and slept with our feet facing each other. I had a little bit of pot left, so I chewed on some stems while drinking some of the whiskey I'd picked up earlier that afternoon. I got a few bottles to avoid any more disasters like the night before. I caught a pretty good buzz, which helped drown out some of the considerable noise from the other campers—and allowed me to avoid stuffing those dirty things back in my ears—and fell asleep on top of my sleeping bag.

I woke up during the night, freezing my ass off. The temperature had dropped considerably. It was probably in the forties, and I was wearing nothing but a pair of red mesh shorts. I put on a hoodie and sweatpants, then wrapped up in my sleeping bag and went back to sleep. But I kept waking up from shivering so much.

When the morning came, I was still shivering. I put on several layers of clothes and kept them on even when the afternoon got into the high eighties. Everyone else was in shorts and T-shirts, while I felt like I was in downtown Buffalo in the early winter. I knew this was punishment for not swerving the night before. Wherever I looked, I saw that poor little skunk oozing all over the road.

Ian and I went to see Old Faithful, and I wanted to jump inside to heat up. After, we checked out some of the other geysers and walked a few trails, then went back to the tent. We started talking with some cute girls in the site beside ours, but that ended quickly when they started calling us fags for sharing a tent. We'd planned to hit another trail, but instead Ian drove us to a sporting goods store and insisted I buy my own tent.

"This is fucking crazy, man. You made me leave mine in Buffalo. Now I've gotta buy another one?"

"Fuck, maybe you are a fag."

"I'm not a fucking faggot!"

I bought the cheapest tent they had, and then Ian insisted I buy a new sleeping bag as well because mine was "too fucking heavy." Considering the chill I'd felt the previous night, I didn't put up much resistance and bought one that was supposed to be good down to ten degrees Fahrenheit. When we got back to the campsite, instead of making me throw out my old sleeping bag like he said he would, Ian watched me put it in my new tent without saying anything. I figured I'd use the old one to sleep on and the new one to keep warm.

The cute girls were gone, but I was glad to get some space from Ian. Still, though, the tent and bag set me back another hundred and fifty bucks. I'd cashed in some of my savings bonds before leaving Buffalo and had already blown through half of what was supposed to last me our seven-week trip.

I'd hoped to put it off longer, but I was so cold that I ended up grabbing some quarters and taking a nearly half-hour-long shower with the water as hot as it'd go. I could feel my core temperature rising, and soon I was back to normal. It felt great to be clean, but I knew I'd be dirty again in no time, and washing took such strength, focus, and energy that cleanliness depressed the hell outta me. To get clean, you had to remember to buy soap and then remember where you'd put it when you needed it. Then you'd have to grab it and find the shower, despite all the chaos and screaming and filth surrounding you, then hope a shower was free. If not, you had to wait. Maybe someone else would take the shower when it was your turn and then you'd have to wait again and then someone else would take it from you once more. Maybe there'd be no hot water left when it was my turn, and then, right when I'd flip on the water, he'd start screaming at me to turn it off because he didn't want me to waste anymore goddamned water. Even if everything worked out perfectly and I had my soap and shampoo and hot water, perhaps someone would drag me out of there while I was washing—or maybe they'd drag a crocodile or some snakes inside, and they'd start snapping at me while I was shampooing and had my eyes closed. Maybe girls would come inside and see me naked and take pictures and post them up next to the pictures of buffalos goring people. Or maybe little girls would come in, and I'd have to scream at them to leave, and their fathers would hear and drag me out to a field and rip the life from my body. Maybe I'd slip and fall and snap my neck and no one would help me. Or what if the thoughts came back? What if they made me keep scrubbing and scrubbing and scrubbing until I wore holes in my skin? Until people started to crowd around and point and laugh and throw shit at me. What if I couldn't wash away the contamination? What if it followed me back to camp and I infected everyone else? Would that make me a murderer? Would they finally stick my ass in prison where I belonged? In the fucking nuthouse? Fuck washing. Fuck drying. It was all so depressing. So impossible. My body was nothing more than a host for fungus. My mind nothing more than blank canvas for evil to paint on. Fuck it all. . . .

We hiked a nearby trail, then came back to the campsite and ate SpaghettiOs for dinner. We washed it down with some beer, popped some of the pills the dudes from Kentucky gave me, and passed the fuck out. I wanted to be out cold enough that I wouldn't wake up should a grizzly start gnawing on the back of my head.

Sometime in the middle of the night, however, I woke up with an overwhelming urge I couldn't ignore. I was dreaming of Delilah. We were both naked, and I was straddling her huge tits as she massaged lotion all over my hard dick. She had this look on her face, begging me to cum all over it.

I unzipped my tent and went to the bathroom, thinking the whole way of that beautiful face and those huge tits. I'd met Delilah at a bar a few months before graduation. Her name was actually Mandy, but everyone called her Delilah for some reason. She bumped into me while dancing and spilled my drink. But I didn't care. She looked up at me with these big, dark eyes, as if to say, "I'm sorry," and just then I'd have forgiven her for lopping off my leg. We started talking, and she had the best things to say. She wasn't like the others—dull, lifeless conversations about current pop stars, or horrible professors, or the best/worst frats. . . . She spoke about poetry and travel and film. We continued the conversation on the way to her apartment, which was right above the bar. Her roommates weren't home, so she had no problem ripping off her clothes the moment she shut the door. I did the same, and we kissed slowly and heavily while grabbing all over one another. She led me to her room and pushed me onto her bed. I could tell she was ready for more, but I didn't want to push it. Sex had a time limit. Sex had politics and expectations. And I just wanted to share the moment with her. To kiss her and feel her energy, her spark, long into the morning hours. She didn't have a full bush, but it certainly wasn't trimmed, which made me think that she probably hadn't been out cruising for sausage that night. That, perhaps, maybe we really had a connection? Because of the band, I'd been with enough other girls it was making me sick. But I liked her. I liked kissing Delilah. I liked holding her. I liked looking up and seeing her room decorated with posters of old French films and photos of trips to foreign museums and paintings she'd likely done herself. I could feel her grinding on me, begging to take it inside. But even though I'd already popped my cherry about a month back after holding off for so long due to all the Thou Shalt Nots!, I didn't want to ruin the moment, and we kept kissing until sunlight filled her room. When we got up, she made me breakfast, and we watched *City of God*. It was one of the most beautiful mornings I'd ever had, and when the time came, I didn't want to leave. I wanted to move in. I wanted to stay in her arms forever, warm and safe. The bar below was calling for my soul, but up there, with her, I'd be all right.

But I wasn't all right, and I fucked it all up. One night while we were at a bar together, I felt the urge to piss. The place wasn't busy yet, so the guy's room probably wasn't full, but even so, the thought of going in there and pissing in that trough while frat assholes chanted and cheered behind me caused me to panic. So, feeling good in that moment, I whipped it out, leaned forward, and pissed on the bar while still maintaining conversation. The bouncer saw and bounced my ass, despite Delilah's protests (she hadn't seen anything). We got separated, and I ended up going home with another girl. The next week, I also hooked up with one of Delilah's friends after a show. I didn't like these other girls. I'd have crawled through a field of thumbtacks just to touch Delilah. But I'd gone home with these girls anyway. I hated them. I hated me. I hated sex. I hated love.

Delilah was one of the few girls who'd come to our shows and actually be present. She'd comment on song lyrics or chord changes or particular sounds that moved her, while the other girls sloshed around, puking and pissing all over everything good in the world. Every time we played "Up on Cripple Creek," I was singing to her. God, how she lifted me. My Delilah was beautiful. But I was ugly, and Ian was wrong to say she wasn't good enough for me. I wasn't good enough to clean her puke. She was there with another guy the night I saw Matt and Zach playing with their new band. I woke up the next morning lying in a muddy field beside the highway.

But she came back to me that cool, mountain night. In my dream, I was between her huge tits, massaging in and out. I almost jizzed in my pants on the shuffle to the bathroom, and when I got there and locked myself in a stall, I hardly even touched it before I erupted like Old Faithful. I felt another urge and sat just in time to pass a decade's worth of filth through me. This time, it didn't even sting. It was as if the gods were finally giving me one. Every so often life shifted in the favor of even the biggest drunk or most crooked grifter, and I accepted this gift without question. I went back to my tent and fell into a deep sleep.

"Yo, if you're not packed up and ready in five minutes, I'm leaving your ass."

I opened my tent and saw Ian standing by the car, his tent and gear already put away. I checked the time: six thirty.

"Why are we leaving so early?" I said.

"Four minutes and thirty seconds."

"Fuck this." But I packed up my shit quickly and made it out of there in time. I drove again. We headed northwest, and when we crossed into Montana, I was hit with nostalgia. As a kid, I had world map sheets and a US map pillowcase, and I'd spend hours on weekend mornings studying them. Something about Montana always called to me. Also, when we were little, my brother and I played a game where we tried to find license plates from all fifty states, and we found all but Montana. Now, here I was, Montana license plates everywhere. This truly felt like the Wild West.

We stopped at a sporting goods store in Bozeman and impulsively bought hoodies and Bozeman hats, then continued northwest through Butte and up to Kalispell. Somewhere along the way we drove alongside a train cutting through the vast countryside, which alternated dusty browns and rich greens and blues. We were both in a race, speeding along to Blue-Skied Freedom, but the car was running low on gas, so I pulled into a gas station and parked next to some big bikers with US flags hanging behind their Harleys. The train kept going. The bikers stared us down. I got a weird feeling there, like anything could happen at any time—a feeling I'd only felt while traveling through Mississippi.

Apparently, to some people, having New York plates and long hair was an invitation to fuck with you. They started catcalling us. I could tell Ian wanted to beat some ass, but I told him to ignore it, and we took off for another gas station. I didn't want to get buried behind some Unabomber shack in the mountains. While I pumped gas, Ian opened the trunk, revealing a huge cooler filled with ice.

"What the fuck, man?"

"It's my car."

"I thought ice was too heavy?"

"Shut the fuck up and pump gas, bitch."

All he had in the cooler were three water bottles.

"Yo, can I at least get one of those? I'm out of water, and I don't want to have to buy more."

"Fuck that. These are mine."

"Well, you probably pissed in 'em anyways, so fuck it."

I bought a gallon of water, paid for the gas, and we took off. It was hot as fuck again, but the dry air felt good as we cruised along. We passed a small airport, and I considered checking on any flights back to Buffalo or Rochester or even New York. I had just enough cash left for a ticket. Now was the point of no return. But I kept driving, and soon we arrived in Glacier National Park. At the gate, Ian requested a second park map after they handed me one. We both wanted them as souvenirs.

We found our campsite, set up our tents, and went into town for some pizza and beer. When we finished eating, we went to a bar that had stuffed animal heads all over the wooden walls. We splurged for some Sierra Nevada Pale Ales and talked to some cute girls who'd been giving us the eye. Ian did most of the talking. I wasn't good with girls. If I knew a girl, I had no problems talking with her, but in situations like this, I never knew what to say. Besides, we were too far from Conesus for me to have a shot—but maybe it was better that way. When we were in the band, it was easy. Girls who'd once given me the cold shoulder would come up to me. Tell me I was cute. Tell me their friend thought I was cute, and wouldn't I go talk to her? I couldn't say no. It was rude. It wasn't allowed. My sexuality wasn't mine—it never was. My body belonged to everyone and no one at once. And I don't think I even knew what sexuality was to begin with. Thou Shalt Not! Blessed Be To Those Who Say No! Sex was painful. It hurt to cum. It was all so much work, and for what? Sweat, blood, pain. Even if I wasn't attracted to a girl, I performed. Even if she made me sick. Time after time, I'd wake up in her bed. Each time, I felt more and more disgusted with myself. One morning, I woke up and started slapping myself hard in the face as the girl ran off in horror. So instead, I stopped showering. Stopped using deodorant. Stopped washing my hair. Sometimes four, five, six days—a week or more—without washing. But that didn't stop them. They kept coming. Kept sucking on my filth. Kept licking up my disease. I knew they could smell it on me. And some of these girls were good girls too. Church girls. Future teachers and doctors and scientists. And they all tasted my filth. Our filth. . . ? Some came back for more. They didn't even want me, just some image of me—a guy on stage in Cow Country, NY. People only wanted what they could understand, and growing up in the US, they knew that anyone on a stage deserves to have their genitals licked. All I wanted was Delilah. To just sit beside her and watch TV. To make her dinner. Listen to her talk about her latest painting or the new steps she learned in her dance troupe. Write her songs and play them for her before bed. But she faded away, and who could blame her? That night I saw her out with the other guy, I drank enough to never wake up. We still talked a little after graduation, but never like we did before. I knew I'd fucked it up. Knew, as I was pissing on that bar, that I'd never be able to stop it. I couldn't stop anything—was just storming forward—ever forward, rolling, rolling, rolling into a sunset of ash and smoke.

"So, you're a teacher?" the cute girl said.

"Oh, uh, no . . . no." I put my beer on the bar and hid in the bathroom for a good fifteen minutes. When I returned to the bar, the girls were gone.

Ian and I walked beside a lake with an incredible view of the mountains just beyond. The sun had already set, but there was still enough warm light to see far into the horizon. We sat on a picnic table and stared at the smooth rocks under the crystal-clear water.

"Yo, man, what's your deal with girls?" Ian said.

"I don't even know. When I like a girl, I end up fucking everything up, so why even let it get that far? Besides, nobody knows anybody. Nobody knows anything."

"You'll find the right girl one of these days. Just wait 'til we get down to Mexico. If you can't fall in love there, there's something wrong with you. Mexican girls are the most beautiful in the world, and they're so sweet and caring."

"Yeah, maybe . . . Hey, you hear from Doug at all?"

"Yeah, he called me the other day. He's on tour right now, playing some big shows. I checked to see if any'd overlap with our trip, but he's on the East Coast now."

"That's fucking great. I'd love to go on tour too, but

I don't think I have it in me. I couldn't even hack it in our shitty band."

"Yo, you're way better than those guys."

"Who? Matt and Zach?"

"Yeah. I mean, not at guitar—Zach fuckin' shreds, man. But your songs are on a different level. They write stuff that's catchy and melodic and clean, even when it's rough. But your stuff is dripping. I mean, it's fucking dripping and coats everything it touches. You write from a different place than they do. They'll always have jobs as studio musicians or whatever. But you got something else."

"Maybe, but they dumped my ass."

"They were planning to get back together with their old band all along—long before we even started playing. It was bound to happen sooner or later."

"Really?"

"Yeah, I mean, they only asked me to play bass 'cause their bassist joined some reggae group in New York."

"Fuck! Why didn't you say yes?"

"I'm not really into their style. They're fucking great musicians, but it's just not my thing. Besides, I can't wait to get down to Mexico. I'm tellin' you, man, Mexico's where it's at."

"Yeah, I can't wait."

"Plus, they're fuckin' junkies."

"What?"

"Yeah, I saw 'em shoot up before a few shows."

"What the fuck?"

"I just don't wanna be around that shit."

"Christ, I didn't know that."

"I couldn't take any more of those shows we played either. Those were the worst."

70

"Yeah, they sucked ass."

"The audiences were always terrible. Most of those people weren't even there for the music. They just wanted to get fucked up and find someone to lick their junk."

"That shit was killin' me. I don't even know why."

"You'll find your audience one of these days."

"If the bears don't get me first."

"Sorry, but if I see a bear, I'm stabbin' your ass and running like hell."

We both laughed.

"Still, though, there was something beautiful in it," I said.

"In what?"

"In playing those shows. A part of me was ready to give it all away with every song."

"See, that's your problem, man. You romanticize all this shit. You do the same with girls. Nobody even gives like a hundredth of a fuck about this stuff that you do—no, maybe a fuckin' thousandth. You're bleeding for everyone and everything, and they don't give a fuck about you."

"Well, maybe I'm not the problem. . . ."

"Yo, fuck Delilah, fuck the band, fuck all that shit. Think about this—I really want you to think about it. Right now, Matt and Zach are probably rockin' a huge fucking room. Right now, Delilah is probably blowin' some dude. Right now, Doug's voice is coming through thousands of stereos. That shit's happening. It's fucking real. What are *you* doing?"

We got up early the next morning and took off for the Hidden Lake Trail. I drove us through the park and up Going-to-the-

Sun Road, a narrow, winding, fifty-mile road built along the mountains with a gorgeous view of the park. As incredible of a drive as it was, with every mile further, I became more terrified. The guardrails were minimal or nonexistent, and the car's brakes had already been almost worn away. On top of that, I had a pretty crippling fear of heights and didn't trust myself not to freak out and accidentally drive us over the cliff to our deaths. So I kept my eyes up and tried to enjoy the view. We passed over the Continental Divide, back into the eastern section, and made it to the trail about two hours after we'd left camp. There were signs everywhere warning visitors to watch out for bears. This was prime grizzly country, and other visitors had been hurt or killed. With the proper precautions, the risk of attack went down, but any risk was too much for me. After spending a lifetime trying to convince myself my inner risks weren't real, I was terrified to be in a place where the risks were now printed on grizzly-shaped posters.

As Ian and I started on the nearly three-mile hike, it calmed me to see so many other visitors along the trails, but eventually the other potential bear-snacks filtered away. We walked a winding gravel trail with mountain goats watching us from a distance, and we stopped every so often to run and jump into fields of snow and ice. My knees began to ache, but I continued. There was no way Ian was stopping for anything short of having his legs hacked off, and even then he'd start dragging himself along with his arms. Eventually, we made it to a large clearing where Hidden Lake opened up in the distance. God, it was perfect—the deepest blue surrounded by evergreens, and above, jagged, snowy mountains.

"What would you do if we saw a moose carcass when we got down there?" Ian said.

"Slowly back away, then run like hell."

We took a trail through short evergreens and arrived at the lake. I started stripping down and approached the water but stopped when I heard something moving through the trees. As much as I'd wanted to have that lake to myself, I was relieved to see a young French couple, and not a bear, approach us. I put my clothes back on, and we hiked back to the parking lot. I was thankful to have survived the hike but still nervous about that narrow mountain road. Trips like these always filled me with such dread. It was hard enough already just lying in my tent, but add any extra risk—any extra surprises—and the floodgates opened all the way, filling me with chemicals that strangled my body and mind. I'd get dizzy and confused and angry and nervous, and the light burned my eyes, and my back and knees ached, and I'd get giddy and goofy and would say and do dumb things. It was best to avoid the trails. Best to stay in the tent. But as much as my body ached from the pain, it ached even more to see all the beauty out there. To hit every trail at once. But I knew this would only spread me thinner and thinner until there was nothing left. Disappearing little by little. Sacrificing it all on an endless quest for beauty and purity. Staying or going, I was doomed—in pain. Always in pain. I knew, though—just knew—that someday there'd be a reward for having endured it all. I just hoped it'd come soon. It had to come soon. I didn't have much time left.

Despite the anxiety, the ride back was peaceful and seemed much shorter than the trip there. We crossed back over the Continental Divide, back into the Snowy West, and stopped at a convenience store to get some grub. While browsing the drinks in the refrigerator section, I glanced at Ian and could see the haste in his eyes as he grabbed a few bags of chips and some water, then got in line. I knew something was up, so I grabbed a drink and a loaf of bread, and hurried toward the line, but just before I got there, an older man ambled in front of me. Fuck! Ian paid and took off. The man in front of me took his sweet time counting the exact change for his purchase.

Outside, I wasn't the least bit surprised to see the car gone. Oh, that motherfucker! That stupid piece of shit! I walked back the two miles to our campsite, where he was sitting on the picnic table and playing his guitar. He turned and gave a fake-ass smile.

"Oh, hey, man, such a great night, don't you thi—"

"What the *fuck* is your problem?"

"Oh, that's it—" He got up, set down his guitar, and approached me as if to start swinging. "Yo, you're such a fuckin' little bitch. Always wasting everybody's time. I should beat your fuckin' ass! I should cut you in your sleep!"

"I-I don't get it. I just don't get it. What do you even want?"

"I wanna toss your bitch ass off a cliff."

"This trip was supposed to be about freedom. Experience. But it's been nothing but a nightmare."

"You're free to leave if you don't like it."

"Maybe I will."

"If you do, I'm sellin' your shit."

I ate some SpaghettiOs for dinner, then took a walk. I came across a group of people sitting on wooden benches and listening to a park ranger speak about the park. I took a seat somewhere in the back. The ranger was in her early thirties, and she had the kindest air about her. She told us about the park's history and the importance of conservation and some interesting experiences she'd had there. One night while backcountry camping, she'd watched as a pack of twenty or so wolves took on a grizzly, and the grizzly straight up demolished them. Her every word seemed elevated, as if coming from a better place. She clearly loved her job. She clearly loved nature. Sitting there in that calm, cool, crisp night, under the careful watch of the bright, warm stars, I felt safe for the first time in a long time. Her knowledge soothed me. Her passion invigorated me. But it also reminded me of how long a journey I'd need to take to arrive at that same place. I had such serious problems learning. Some things came to me easily, but others hurt my brain so much, I just couldn't understand them—even if they were as basic as "put the yellow paper in the yellow folder." I was always leaping from idea to idea, thought to thought, and could never concentrate on anything long enough to really understand it. I'd never be able to stay in one place like this woman and learn everything about it and love it and feel it and share it with the world. I wished she'd just reach out and touch me and make everything okay. That she'd give me the gift of peace and knowledge. But I felt so out of place around these people. So out of place around real adults who had real jobs and wore real adult clothes and knew exactly what they'd be eating for dinner that night and where all their utensils were and could clean those utensils and put them away, then read a book before bed without wanting to blow out their fucking brains.

I was burning up. A fucking wildfire out of control. The thought of working a normal job, then coming home and cooking a fucking chicken dinner seemed as impossible as growing wings out of my ass and flying off into space. I was both drawn to and repulsed by these types of crowds. They made cleaning look so easy. They made learning look so easy. Made raising children look so easy. I couldn't even take a shit without the whole fucking world caving in on me. Couldn't even shower without the soap and water stinging my ass and brain. I drank and I did drugs, and these people were absolutely certain that those who drank and did drugs were bad. They were the Devil. They deserved Kurt Cobain's fate. I envied the peace these people seemed to feel, but it was clear to me that it would never be mine, and they'd never take the time to show me how to have it. They just did, and I just didn't, and as much as I wanted to sit there and be at peace with all of them, another part of me wished a pack of wolves would move in and rip them all to shreds. The wolves would leave me alone. I knew that for certain. All that pain and torment assured me that much at least. Here, in the wild, I was king. Still, I just wanted peace. Christ, at least it was nice getting away from Ian for a while. Why'd you even tell him you might leave? You know it's all bullshit. You know you can't stop. Besides, going back to Buffalo will be the same shit. Coming or going, I'm fucked. So, going it is. . . .

When I got back to the campsite, Ian was already asleep. I went to my tent and pulled out both books I'd brought with me: a biography of Napoleon and *Big Sur* by Jack Kerouac. This trip was equal parts Napoleon and Kerouac, but Kerouac was already everywhere around me, so I went with Napoleon. I drank a few beers and got through about twenty pages before the headache was too much. I went to sleep.

"Yo, the car's leaving with or without you!"

Christ, not again. . . . I checked my watch: five thirty

a.m. What the fuck? I unzipped my tent. "Why, man? Why?"

"Just get moving."

I packed everything up and put it in the car. "Can I at least brush my teeth?"

"No, we gotta go."

Jesus fucking christ.

We drove to a Laundromat outside of the park. We met two other guys about our age also washing their clothes.

"We're almost done with our trip now. What's it been, eight weeks?" one said.

"I think nine now," the other said.

"What about you guys?" the first said.

"I think it's been about two weeks," I said.

"Man, you guys are gonna have such a great time. There's still so much out there to see," the second one said.

"Yeah," Ian said.

"How's it been so far?"

"Insane," I said.

"That's dope, bro. . . ."

Even so early in the morning, they looked to be having a great time. They'd grown out their beards and had gotten matching tattoos in Seattle. Meanwhile, I was surprised Ian and I hadn't killed one another yet, and we'd only been on the road for a fraction of the time.

We took off when our clothes were dry. Ian drove us west through the Rockies. Northern Idaho was achingly beautiful, but all that beauty seemed so lonely and sad. I remembered the opium the guys in Colorado had given me "for the right occasion." This seemed about as right as any.

"Wanna smoke?" I said.

"Yeah, sure," Ian said.

I packed my bowl, hit it, and was immediately overcome with a relaxing, yet still ominous, feeling. An hour later, the bright green trees and clear blue sky had all become shimmering crystals. It was pretty, but there seemed to be some deception about them. The drug altered my perception of nature, and I realized that I preferred nature alone, without the drugs. Preferred nature even with all its bears and wolves and flying squirrels. Why'd I smoke this? Fuck, don't you realize this is the shit heroin's made out of? You've just crossed a serious bridge. Broken down a steel-reinforced concrete wall. Just a slip and a tumble to the needle now. Nature alone just wasn't good enough for ya, huh? I'm gonna punish your ass for this. You'd better believe I'm gonna punish your ass.

But I had to do it. And it's not so bad. A little more powerful than weed. Got a great taste and smell. Maybe they'll all respect me a little more now. I can't handle the psychedelics like they all can. I can't handle meth like Tania and Nikki. I'm a pussy. A long-haired charlatan. You're no hippy. You're just a scared-stupid white boy from Buffalo. You're no musician. No songwriter. Bowie, Dylan, Lennon, Lou Reed, Jim Carroll all shot H. You're just a bitch. You don't belong, man. You can buy tickets to the show, but you'll never be onstage. Go stand somewhere in the back and stay outta the way. Music's for the big leaguers. Matt and Zach shoot H. Doug Morricone drops acid and smokes crack. Kurt, Layne, Scott all shot H. You can't even take a shit if someone outside is laughing. You'll never be able to write songs until you can just man the fuck up. Maybe if I just shoot up, it'll unlock that gate and allow me to finally see that beauty inside of me. Maybe artists are supposed to burn out. To sacrifice it all for their work. After all, the work lasts forever. But no one's body does, no matter how often they go to church, or how many vegetables they eat. Heroin, man. Just a small step from here. But I'm not really feeling any gates unlocking now. Maybe I need something stronger? At least I can now cross opium off my list. At least I've finally done a real drug. If anyone asks, I won't sound as much like a pussy. "Oh, acid? No thanks, but you got any opium?" "Oh, yeah, well I've done shrooms and opium." "Yeah, opium gives you a nice, mellow high. Better than weed, that's for sure." Christ, I was surrounded by nature but felt so far from it. Ian was cruising along, not saying shit. We were listening to Ween, "She Wanted to Leave." Such a beautiful song. Simple yet so powerful. I could write this story. I've lived this story. Why don't words like this just come to me? I'd get half a verse before the whole thing disappeared. Try heroin, man. You're the only bitch who hasn't done it yet. Do you wanna be a bitch forever?

But, fuck, man, I'm not like all the others. All the others seem okay to stand and talk and drink and smoke without the life being strangled from them. All the others seem cool to talk to girls and take road trips and be happy and do their laundry and eat bagels and smile. All the others seem like they can cook a fucking chicken, then take a shit and shower and go out for a night on the town without daggers in their guts and vise grips on their brains. I'd felt the strangle of insanity clamping around me a few times throughout my life. I knew what it felt like. It hit me hard as a kid. The demands. The rituals. The obsessions. The hours of prayers. Dirty ear plugs in my ears. Hours and hours and hours a day wasted on nothing. Thoughts racing but going nowhere. Then there were the Evil Thoughts . . . all on top of the screaming and smashing and ass-beatings. . . . The stress pushed me over a few times. You have no idea how powerful your brain is until it turns on you. Your brain is everything. Trust me. It's everything. There's nothing more isolating than insanity. You're isolated even from yourself— slipping deeper and deeper inside, yet further and further away. Everything—sights, sounds, smells—reminds you of the reality you're leaving behind, and the sound of people laughing and talking about dinner and making plans for the future just drives you further over the edge. The smell of food. Even oxygen burns your skin. And no one can help you—not that they even would. The fear is crippling and only makes it all worse. Some people have probably reached their limit and think they know what it feels like, but when you really go over, when you've hit that point where return is impossible . . . that's insanity—knowing you're stuck and that no one can do a thing about it. Luckily, each time I snapped back in, but if someone had dosed my ass or had blown a puff of marijuana smoke in my face at that moment, maybe I'd have drifted off forever. And once you've gone over, a part of you never comes back—it's just over there, waiting for the rest of you to return. I knew I was going to go insane one of these days and I needed to get the music and poetry out of me first. But the more I pursued these, the crazier I felt. So I remained in limbo—never doing, never not-doing. Just floating, from place to place, person to person, orgasm to orgasm. Twenty-seven was coming. Twenty-one already came and went—I'd already overstayed my welcome. Before I went, though, I wanted to share my beauty with the world. It'd make the whole struggle worth it. It'd make death feel honorable. And heroin, to me, was death. And now I was knocking on its door.

It started to wear off around the time we got to the Cascades, which gave us some relief from the dry Eastern Washington heat. I was thrilled to cross the Columbia River, which, to me, felt like the last natural barrier between us and California. Once we passed over the Cascades, we rolled down into Seattle. By the time we got to the city, I was feeling like myself again.

Coming from Buffalo, this place seemed so foreign. Cozy Craftsmans and minimalist modern houses littered the city's fringes, and the whole place stunk of real wealth—not Buffalo wealth. Not both-of-my-parents-are-lawyers wealth, but millionaire and billionaire meeting-with-world-leaders kinds of cash. It made me feel ashamed of my dirty, ripped clothes and the shitty car we were driving.

We found a hostel downtown and paid to sleep in a huge dormitory-style room with about twelve other people—and one fucking bathroom. Shit! We chose our beds—a set of bunk beds in the far corner—and got some pizza at a nearby spot. When we came back to the room, it was filled with other guests. The first we spoke to were a short, thin Irish boxer and a tall, muscular Korean who'd just finished his term with the Republic of Korea Army Special Forces. The four of us went up to the bar on the roof for some drinks, and the two tough guys scanned the crowd and discussed how they'd take out the various people surrounding us, should they attack. Ian played along a bit, but I think even he knew he was outmatched, so he eventually shut the fuck up. I started talking to two Mexican girls from Compton, and Ian joined me. I kinda liked the one girl. She was pretty and had a great body, and she was really into dance. I loved dancers. Girls who knew how to move their bodies. Probably because all of my energy was always pulling so strongly inward, I was attracted to those whose energy was more kinetic. We danced for a bit, and she kissed me all over my neck and cheeks. Soon the other friend came over, said something to my girl, and the two left. Ian and I had a few more drinks, then went downstairs and climbed into our beds. It was dark and everyone seemed to be sleeping, except for one couple I could definitely hear fucking.

When she stopped moaning, I figured I'd give it a try. I started pulling down my pants before I got to the bathroom, then ripped them off once I'd shut and locked the door; I sat and immediately started giving it hell. My stomach was killing me, and I needed to get rid of everything in it. I started to get the feeling and all systems were preparing for release, but someone's bed squeaked and I completely lost it. No! Please, no! I've gotta go so badly. . . . I started pulling inward, always inward, and the feeling disappeared, forever kept inside where everything turned to shit. I started pushing as hard as I could, but nothing. I got up and took a long look at myself in the mirror. I could hear the boxer and Special Forces guy coming back in the room, talking about how they'd take down famous leaders throughout history, and I burst into tears. I mean, I was fucking weeping. Hold it in. Hold them back. Don't let them hear you crying. Boys Don't Cry! Boys Don't Feel Pain! They put Mussolini in a headlock and gouge out his eyes. Boys shit wherever they feel like it. Boys come and see and conquer. Wipe your tears on a towel so they don't see them on your shirt. You can't go back out there like this. Those dudes will turn on you next.

I was wiping away my tears with a towel when someone tried to open the door. I jumped and accidentally dropped the towel in the toilet. I fished it out, tossed it in the garbage, washed my hands, and went back to bed. I could hear the couple starting in on round two.

I had them with me—always with me—but I didn't put them in my ears. Just don't do it, man. Better to beat it back with whiskey. I did shots until I passed out. Shots until I passed out. Shots until I passed out. I passed out with shots.

I woke up late the next morning and, for some reason, was the only one in the room. That might have seemed like a good time to try to use the bathroom, but that was exactly why it was the worst. It had to be done during an off-moment, when I wasn't thinking about it. Just sneaking up on the shit and pushing it out. And these quiet moments brought too much time to think—too much pressure. No, now was the time for something else.

I pulled out my music and played "I'm on Fire" by Bruce Springsteen. There was something so intimate about hearing that song in that shared yet empty room—some special connection between him and me. It was one of my mother's favorites. She and I had both been through so much. We'd both been on fire, but hers had gone out so long, long ago. I wished she knew how much I loved her. How much I wanted her to be happy. But, because of that desire, how badly it hurt me to be around her. I wished she knew how beautiful she was, despite all the shit he screamed at her. Maybe, if she already knew, I wouldn't have to go out searching on all these lonely dangerous roads in an endless quest to bring beauty back home to her. Thank you, Bruce, for giving her something so powerful. For making her feel beautiful. For making her believe someone out there was still burning for her. Thank you for giving me something so powerful as well. Though brief, listening to that song on the top bunk in an empty dorm-style Seattle hostel made me feel as though everything was gonna be all right. As though Bruce and I had written that song together to save the world. As though it was a guide to better things, better days.

Soon, two of the guests showed up, and I was glad I'd used that moment for music and not more shit.

Ian came back too. "Yo, get your shit and let's get outta here."

"I thought we were staying a few more nights?"

"In Seattle, maybe, but not this shithole. I caught one of these fuckin' Dead Heads washing their feet in the sink this morning. I'm not staying here another minute."

"Where we gonna go?"

"Anywhere, man. Let's just get there."

I packed up and we piled into the car and took off. The streets were hilly and I could hear the last of the brakes wearing away. Ian pulled out his phone as he drove. "Hey, Ma, I need you to put some more cash in my bank account . . . What the fuck do you mean? I don't give a shit—whatever you gotta do . . . Jesus christ, all right already . . . Yo, are you gonna give it to me or not?"

I stared at the Seattle skyline, into Elliott Bay, down the alleys, and under the bridges where the ghosts slept . . . waiting . . . watching. . . .

"Christ, that wasn't so hard, was it?" Ian hung up and turned into the first motel parking lot we saw. "Damn, she drives me fucking crazy."

"How much she give you?"

"Enough to cover the next few nights."

"Tell her I said thanks."

"Yeah, whatever. . . ."

We got a room on the second floor, dropped our things, and took off. On the way down the hall, we passed an open door. Inside, three guys were rubbing all over a half-naked girl, who looked to be about seventeen.

"Hey, you guys wanna hit this first?" one of the guys said to us.

"Yeah, man, she got a nice big ass," another said. He slapped it.

"Come on now, sweetie," she said. "I told you already, you all wanna ride the train, you all gotta buy a ticket. And only one of you's done that so far." She smiled through it all with the kind of poise only a girl in her line of work could possess.

I followed Ian into the room. The guys crowded around her, forcing her into a corner.

"Look, we're all gonna fuck you and you're gonna like it," one of the guys said.

"Now, there's no reason to talk like that to a lady," she said.

The guys started laughing.

"A lady?" one said.

There's an opened can of SpaghettiOs on the counter. Someone could cut themselves on the lid. . . .

"Damn right a lady."

Someone could get hurt. . . .

"I wanna get the ass."

Should I walk over and put the lid down?

"No way, the ass is all mine."

No, that's rude, right? You can't just touch someone else's can without their permission.

"Fuck you, take it then."

Ian started backing away. "Yo, let's get the fuck outta here."

I didn't need much convincing.

"You can both have the ass, I just need to see some loot."

We walked down the hall and out into the cool Seattle haze. We were close to the downtown party scene, so we went on foot. Walking in any new place usually caused the chemicals to surge and my muscles to squeeze like hell, and that afternoon was no exception. It only worsened as we passed street after street filled with kids our age or younger playing guitar or drumming sticks on plastic buckets or asking if we wanted any hash or if we had any extra change. Dirty, burned-out ghosts breezing from one spot to the next. I could feel his ghost too—their ghosts, haunting those streets. I could feel his death dripping from the air. He'd killed himself right around the time the Evil Thoughts came on, and while I didn't blame him for these thoughts, his death did remind me of my own. Things were happy. They were pretty good at some point, until they weren't. After he died, they all called him the Devil. He was Satan trying to pull kids down into hell with him. A guitar-wielding Pied Piper, leading us all astray. From early on, I knew music was evil. Rock 'n' roll was Satan himself. The nuns all said so. And they were good. So it had to be true. They held the key to heaven. And I couldn't go to hell. I'd never last there. I could hardly last here. When I died, Kurt died; when Kurt died, I died. We died together. I killed him. He killed me. We were both dead, haunting the streets of Seattle. And when I died, I couldn't even tell anybody. When I spoke like this, they all told me I was weird—nuts. They told me to shut up. They hit me. I couldn't speak about music. Couldn't feel it. If I did, they'd banish my ass to hell. And now, the music was stuck in me, building, and building, like the magma under Mount Rainier in the distance. The street kids were everywhere. Far more than I'd ever seen. The West was full of them. Full of broken dreams. Full of shattered lives. The West was . . . a lie. . . ? God, if you stay here too long, maybe it'll get you too. The ghosts infecting your soul. The East is death. The West is sunny death. Just keep moving. Don't think. Keep moving. . . .

We arrived in a posher section of town and stopped in a trendy bar, despite my objections. The people inside were young, sexy, and well groomed. They smelled good, wore clean underwear, and all had dimples. Ian and I were in hoodies and mesh shorts and probably smelled like the back of a Greyhound bus.

"Come on, it's on my mom tonight," he said.

We ordered some craft IPAs and scanned the scene. Everyone was smiling. Everyone was happy. Everyone was shouting. Everyone knew how to dance. Everyone was best friends. Everyone had a house in Tuscany and a yacht in Puget Sound. Everyone got laid three times a day and smiled from the moment they got up in the morning until the time they went to bed at night. I hated them and they hated me. We'd never be able to understand one another, so we did what we always did and ignored each other.

A pretty girl was dancing up a storm in front of us, drawing the attention of every asshole within a ten-foot radius. They were all pumping their fists and chanting and trying to grind on her as she worked herself up into such a self-indulgent trance, light couldn't escape her gravity. Ian started pumping as well. Good luck, homie! You smell like a hobo's ballsack.

She started moving toward us, and the crowd followed. She pushed right between me and Ian, stepping on my foot, and the all-too-eager assholes helped her up on the bar. I'd put my hat up there, and soon she was stomping all over it. "Ex-excuse me." I waved to get her attention, and she gave me a look as if to say, "Stay down there in the pits, pig. Do you know who I am? I'm the Dancing Queen of Seattle." She kicked my hat off the bar, and I bent to pick it up. Guys started surging, pushing up against me, all trying to smack her ass when she bent over. One pinned me against the bar, and I pushed him off.

I grabbed my hat from the floor with one hand and put my other hand on the bar to pull myself back up, and she stomped on my fingers.

"Hey!"

One of the sexy young suitors laughed at me as if to say, *You got no chance, buddy.*

"Hey!" I said again. "Watch what the fuck you're doing!"

She gave me a smirk then kicked my beer off the bar, and I had to fight with everything I had not to grab her leg and pull it out from under her.

"Let's get the fuck outta here," I said to Ian.

"No, man, I think I got a chance." He smiled at her.

She bent over and kissed some dude, who grabbed her and carried her into the crowd.

Ian shrugged, and we pushed outside through the chaos

and left. We stopped in another pizza place with a young street kid playing guitar out front.

"What the fuck is wrong with people? You can't even relax anywhere. You can't set your fucking load down without someone kicking it all over."

"Just relax. You're killin' my buzz."

We found another bar—a dive this time—and filled up on plastic cups of the cheapest swill on tap. I woke up the next morning in the passenger seat of the car, parked in front of our motel room.

Chapter 6

I pushed hard on the brakes, and we slowed to a stop at a mechanic near Mount St. Helens. The guy took a look at the car while Ian and I debated how much we thought it'd cost. Neither of us knew shit about cars, and we prepared to act outraged with whatever price the mechanic quoted us, which came out to be six hundred dollars.

"I gotta say, that sounds steep. My guy back in Staten Island would do it for half that," Ian said.

"Ya need new rotors too."

We continued to play softball, and eventually he said he'd let us camp on his property for free with the price of the job. Even though it seemed like a good deal, we said no. The parking brake was fully functional, and fuck him and everyone else.

We found a campsite near the volcano, set up our tents, and ate some cans of SpaghettiOs for dinner. There were families everywhere, laughing and grilling and fucking with the mood, so I took my guitar down to the small lake behind my tent, sat on the trunk of a fallen tree, and racked my brain for a song. I needed a song. I needed something from this scene. It was so beautiful. The rolling green hills, crystal-clear water, dying orange sun falling through an amber-and-blue sky. This is the spot where Neil Young would say, on some HBO special performance or something, that he got the inspiration to write "Helpless." "Oh, yeah, the rolling green hills, crystal-clear water, dying orange sun falling through an amber-and-blue sky. It just came to me. The water was speaking to me. Birds telling me their secrets. And as I looked up and saw one dying tree in a field of green on a faraway hill, the song just appeared as if to say, don't forget me. Here I am." Then he'd play it for the crowd, and they'd tear up and thank him and tell him how special he was. How dear. This is where Cezanne would see the spheres of stars before they even started to shine. Where Einstein would leap up and say, "Aha! I have it! I have it at last!"

But I was stumped. I put the guitar down and rubbed my feet on the smooth hamburger-shaped rocks below and looked at the horizon where sky, mountain, and lake met. That infinite point where all things came together and existed at once. That infinite point inside of me where art, health, and happiness met. I pulled out my notebook and wrote some words but stopped when a woman's piercing laugh sent shivers through the scene. I remained on that stump long into the night, and when the voices finally died down, I returned to my tent. But I could hear a father somewhere nearby telling his kids ghost stories. I thought of stuffing the plugs in my ears, but instead grabbed some of the beers I'd bought that afternoon and got to work.

I woke up the next morning to more sounds of laughter and good, fatherly advice and hopeful plans for the future. Some people were happy. Some people were happy? I didn't know if they were sincere or simply great actors, but both options terrified me.

"Yo, get your ass moving!"

We drove through the park and saw the volcano, which looked like JFK's dome after the parade, and kept going. The Pacific Northwest was as gorgeous as I'd hoped. Thick trees, blue skies, the heavy scent of fresh nature. I relaxed as we cruised along to some Béla Fleck, but the second we crossed the Oregon state line, I was overcome with a feeling of sheer horror. Can you rape a prostitute? Yeah, you can rape a prostitute. Shit, you can rape anybody. . . .

The speed limit of Oregon was fifty-five. Fuckin' hippy squares. At least the conservative squares let you drive fast as fuck. I drove through Portland, then continued down the 5 with Mount Hood in the distance. Oh, please, lovely mountain, teach me your secret of longevity. About halfway through the state, I drove southwest down some country roads, and soon we arrived at Crater Lake. We drove around the circumference of the lake, looking down at all that ink-blue water, and found a spot to set up camp. By the time we'd pitched our tents, it was too late to hike down to the lake, so we got drunk and played guitar—nothing new, just some old shit we'd played a hundred times before.

The next morning we drove back to the lake, parked, and started hiking down to the water. Crater Lake had been formed when the volcano it's located in, Mount Mazama, blew its lid a few thousand years ago. After, snow and rain filled inside the collapsed volcano, turning it into the deepest lake in the US and one of the clearest in the world. The water was the deepest blue I'd ever seen, and I couldn't wait to get down to it for a closer inspection.

Ian and I took a boat tour of the lake, then hiked back

up the trail. We started the hike together, but when he pulled ahead, I just let him go, knowing what competing with him would bring. When we got to the top, Ian handed me his camera and asked me to snap a shot of him in front of the lake. I took a few shots, then handed him mine and asked him the same, but he refused. "Yo, I'll smash that shit. You're so fucking annoying. Can't you just enjoy one moment without trying to profit from it?" I thought about his words. I didn't know why I was taking pictures other than to show them off to my friends or to prove to skeptics that I'd actually seen these places. Maybe Ian was right. I decided to stop taking pictures for the rest of the trip unless there was a good reason to do so.

We got fucked up again that night and hung out with the two middle-aged women in the spot next to ours. They'd just gotten back from Senegal, where they'd been working with the Peace Corps, and they had a lot of great stories. They told us they were jealous of our youth, and I wanted to tell them I was jealous that they'd survived so long and looked so happy, but I kept my mouth shut. I liked spending time with them, but I returned to my tent, drank some whiskey, and passed out.

Chapter 7

We'd done it! We'd finally passed through the rest of the country, and California was next! I blasted "Englishman in New York" as we neared that beautiful sign and crossed into the Promised Land. I felt the spirits of Woody Guthrie and Kris Kristofferson and Johnny Cash blowing in with us.

This is it, man! This is the place. This is where I'll find my crew. This is where I'll be able to throw off the shackles of student teaching and 1040 tax forms and pleated pants. This is where my band is waiting for me. This is where they'll absorb me into their weird little worlds, and we'll help each other explore the depths of our souls. Where we'll coax the music out of one another. Where they'll see my half-written verses and melodies and find ways to complete them. No, I'll never be lonely again. Never be sad. Here the shit and wine will flow. Here the gods themselves will touch me and make everything okay.

California was foggy and cool. We headed southwest and stopped in Crescent City, a small coastal fishing town. Ian's mom had deposited more cash in his account, so we got a motel room. Neither of us had any interest in ever sleeping in a car again.

We showered, drank some of the beers we'd picked up for cheap at a nearby gas station, and went in search of food. We found an Italian spot, and I scarfed down some lasagna. Then we went to see *Batman Begins*, which had come out a few weeks earlier. I wasn't big on superhero flicks, but after seeing how powerful and gritty Christopher Nolan's take on Batman was, I got into it right away. I knew it was corny as hell, but during the scene where Christian Bale closes his eyes and faces his fears, the bats flying all around him, I closed my eyes and did the same. Even with Ian sitting beside me. I tried to imagine there being nothing he could do—nothing he could say—to shake me off that course. Even if he started stabbing me with his knife or strangling me while screaming in my face. I was the master of this ship. I was in control of my own vehicle.

After the movie, we got another twelve-pack, then went back to the motel and got loaded while watching *Entourage*. I'd never seen it before, so Ian filled me in on all I needed to know. We killed the beers and went to sleep. The room only had one bed, so I slept on top of the covers and Ian under them.

I woke up early that morning and snuck a shit in while Ian was still sleeping. It was a long fight, but I won. The pain wasn't as bad as I'd thought it would be, given how much blood there was, but it still stung for the next few hours as we cruised down the Pacific Coast Highway. Fog, redwoods, sea stacks, salty coast. The brakes were pretty much gone, so I used the emergency brake when taking sharp turns. "When my mom used to live out here, she saw tons of cars lose control and go over these cliffs." Christ, shut the fuck up,

Ian. Occasionally, we'd pass through small neighborhoods, where the houses were quaint, like something out of a fairytale. I figured I'd never even be able to afford to live in one of the toolsheds out back. We stopped for gas, and I felt even more uncomfortable around these people than I had in Montana with the bikers. These people had serious money. These people were players. These people were healthy and happy. These people would be the first to turn on me if they saw the bloodstains in the ass of my mesh shorts. These fuckers would tie me up and send me off to Chino just for looking at their daughters. Just for polluting their air. At least the bikers would just beat my ass and let me be. These fuckers here wanted my soul.

On the way out of the gas station, I saw a hitchhiker about our age standing on the sidewalk, and I immediately looked away. That fucking horrible feeling in my stomach came back. Christ, is it *him*?

I'd spent one rainy late afternoon jamming with Matt and Zach in their living room a few weeks before they got back together with their old band. At our first few shows, we'd played mostly covers, but as time went on, we started playing more and more originals. Most of these were Matt and Zach's, but we worked quite a few of Ian's into our routine too. Though I had songs, I was too afraid to play them. I always felt as though the Darkness and Evil were so tightly wrapped around my tunes that if I started playing them, anyone listening would turn on me in an instant. But something about that living room felt safe, and when the opportunity presented itself, I played a song I'd written about a girl I'd cared deeply for freshmen year. She had a boyfriend who treated her like shit. She'd always tell me how attracted she was to me and how safe and beautiful she felt around me, but no matter how many times she told me she'd leave him for me, she'd always run back to him and ignore me until she needed the emotional support again. Instead of ridiculing me or condemning me to the depths of hell, both Matt and Zach started adding to the tune. It was as if the song already existed, and we were just working through it. We'd been toking most of the afternoon, and I was elevated far above all the shit surrounding me—as if I could finally see everything and it all made sense. It was a powerful moment, seeing those two great musicians take my song so seriously and help me raise it to a place I couldn't bring it to on my own.

And there was a moment when I looked across the room at Matt, who was playing along on an acoustic bass, and I started to feel something else I'd never felt before. There was something about his energy—it felt plugged into my own. While playing this song I'd written about a girl who never cared for me, part of me hoped he'd reach over and touch me. Men weren't supposed to touch you. Men made fun of you. Men made you cry and then made fun of you for crying. Men hit you. Men screamed at you. Men told you music was for faggots. Self-expression was for homos.

But Matt was a man—a manly man. He had a beard; a rugged, muscular chin; a tall, tight body made tough from years of chopping firewood and climbing mountains. I wanted him to touch me. I wanted to feel a connection to another man. To know I wasn't a faggot. I wanted him to touch me so I'd know I wasn't queer. I wanted him to touch me and show me that the music wasn't wrong. Wasn't just for weak men. Zach was there too, but even though he played along, he seemed off in his own world. But Matt—he was right there with me, and I could feel his spirit. There was something so erotic about it. I didn't want his body. I wanted to plug into his soul, his being. He kept such great rhythm. Body powerful but controlled. And I wanted to be under his control. To wrap it around me. Feel it in me. I felt safe in that room. It felt more than sexual. It felt musical.

When the song ended, so did the feeling, and even though I'd never felt anything like that for him—or any other guy—again, that experience fucked me up for a long time after. I wasn't physically attracted to men, but for months, every time I went out and saw some hot girl showing off her tits, I'd immediately think of huge, hard dicks. Whenever a hot girl started rubbing on me, I smelled a man's musk. Whenever a cute girl would bend over, her ass narrowed and became hairy and disgusting. I started to lose connection with both men *and* women. After a few months though, this whole feeling wore away, and I was right back to it again— rubbing all over any girl who'd fallen in with my gravity. But I'd never forget that one afternoon. I don't know what it was that caused me such a strong feeling. Perhaps it wasn't sexuality that caused such a stir, but creativity. Maybe, then, were sexuality and creativity linked somehow? Christ, what more could the exploration of my creativity do to me? What more was I capable of? What other torment. . . ?

This hitcher had the same muscular chin under a thin layer of stubble. That was the first time on the trip I'd felt an ominous feeling about San Francisco. But it was coming up, whether I liked it or not.

Chapter 8

Despite the fog, the Golden Gate Bridge dominated the view ahead. We crossed it, over the bay, speeding right into the heart of our trip. The hilly streets were too much for the car. Even while slamming on the brakes, dropping into neutral, and pulling back on the emergency brake, we still flew right through a red light. Luckily there was no passing traffic. I pulled over at the nearest spot, and Ian called his mom for directions. She sent us first through the Castro, then the Mission, and soon we arrived at the Lower Haight.

We parked, grabbed our bags, and walked east along Buena Vista Park. When we arrived at a corner house, Ian knocked on the downstairs door and was met by a fifty-year-old man, who looked a little like Ernest Hemingway.

"Whoa-ho, that little Ian?" he said. "I haven't seen you since you were runnin' around, pullin' up all the little girls' skirts." He grabbed Ian's shoulders and gave him a playful shove. "Big, solid guy now."

"Hey, Sam," Ian said. "I see you still got the beard."

"It's part of my face. Can't get rid of it."

"Thanks again for lettin' us stay here," Ian said.

"Please, your mother and I used to terrorize these streets together. It's my honor to host her spawn." He shook my hand. "As well as the friends of her spawn. Name's Sam, but you can call me Sam."

"Nice to meet you, Tony," I said.

He laughed. Even with a head full of dynamite, sometimes I still took risks, and it paid off this time.

"This is a great neighborhood," I said.

"This is the *only* neighborhood. Only one left, that is. And it's squeezing tighter and tighter all the time with all them yuppie boutiques and all that crap, but we're fightin' back."

"That's great," I said.

"Where are my manners?" He opened the door and let us inside the small, one-bedroom place. "Come in, come in."

The walls and wooden floor were well worn but still had class. A woman who looked to be in her forties was singing along to, and butchering the hell out of, "Use Me" by Bill Withers, playing on a record player in the dining room. She kept singing and dancing and didn't seem to notice us until she stopped to take a shot of something clear.

"Are these the boys?" She lunged at us and pulled us into a group hug. "The little sweethearts. I bet all the girls love you two."

"This is Ronnie," Sam said. "My best girl."

"Nice to meet you, Ronnie," Ian said. He was the first to pull from her grasp, but I was a close second.

"Man, you boys must be havin' a helluva time! Shit, I crisscrossed the hell outta the country before these titties started saggin' like they do now, and man, I had a great time. Where you comin' from again?"

"Buffalo," Ian said.

"I spent a few weeks in Buffalo, years ago. Came in to see a Rick James show and got lost a few days, know what I mean? That John Fogerty was right. Buffalo's the kinda place to just go, sit by the lake, and take her easy."

"Ronnie's from the East Coast as well," Sam said. He filled a shot glass with tequila and took it down.

"From the Blue Ridge Mountains of North Carolina," she said. "The most beautiful site you ever did see." She grabbed a few more shot glasses, filled them, and handed them over. "Bottoms up, fellas."

"Thanks," I said.

We took the shots, then Sam grabbed some beers from the fridge and passed them around. We sat at the table and caught a nice buzz.

"Man, your mother was a tough gal," Sam said. "Hard to pin down that one."

"Still hard," Ian said.

"Where you guys headed after this?" Ronnie said.

"Los Angel—" I said.

"Mexico," Ian said.

"Meh-hico, huh?" Ronnie said. "Spent a few weeks there too, all up and down the Baja Peninsula. Goddamn it gets hot down there. Melt yer tits right off. I swear, I used ta look like Dolly Parton." She started singing "9 to 5." It didn't sound good.

We ordered a pizza and shot the shit some more. Ian said, "Who wants to hit the town?" but Sam and Ronnie were too tired, so it was just the two of us. We took off walking and passed more street kids and drum circles and small-time dealers, and popped into a few bars on Haight

Street. Ian and I had just ordered bottles of the cheapest beer when "Take Me Out" by Franz Ferdinand came on. Ian's face lost expression. Franz Ferdinand and Doug Morricone had signed with their record labels on the same day. Doug had some big hits but none as big as "Take Me Out." Ian always acted weird when that song came on. I don't know if it was because it pissed him off that this other band had one-upped his buddy, or maybe it reminded him of all the stages he could have rocked, but either way, he'd always stop talking and look as though he were free-falling through a dark void, deeper and deeper into himself.

The song got to me too, but for a different reason. While dicking around at band practice one day, I came up with a riff that was halfway between the one driving "Take Me Out" and another song wildly popular at the time, "Float On" by Modest Mouse. I knew it took more than a fucking riff to make a song, but every time I heard either of those tunes, it reminded me that the whole world was passing me by. Some people felt inspiration and turned it into something beautiful. But me . . . I felt inspiration and ducked for cover. Christ, it was better to not even get the riffs or half verses or incomplete melodies for choruses. Those fucking hurt so bad. They felt like superheated anvils. Burdens. Gardens of darkness. It was best not to think. Best not to feel. Best to put one foot in front of the other. Best to keep moving. Don't think. Drink. Don't think. Smoke. Don't think. Fuck whatever moves. Don't think. Always moving. Always forward. Never backward. Backward is evil. Avoid the evil. Don't think of the evil. The inspiration is down there with all the other horrors. When it pops up, knock it back down. Who knows what might come up with it? Who knows if the Darkness has camouflaged itself as song? Who knows what horrors might be wrapped around those lovely nuggets of sound? If you relax and let it come, you could be summoning Satan. Best to kill it all off. Best to drown it away. Halfway to music is all the way to insanity. All or nothing. Halfway is death. Halfway is prison. I have a nuclear reactor inside of me. An ocean of sound forever crashing against my inner shores. Please, god, take this from me. Please, for once, do something. I just want to teach and be happy. To go out on the weekends in normal places with normal people and sip drinks and talk about the new mall opening up downtown and go home and go to sleep beside my happy wife in our warm happy bed. I'll smile when they smile. Laugh when they laugh. Cry when they cry. Curse out the weirdos and loonies when they do. I could be happy just teaching. No music. No poetry. Just lessons. Just rules. I'll do whatever you say. I'll stop fighting back. . . .

Perhaps it was surrender in Ian's eyes as well whenever that tune came on.

When the song ended, we finished our beers and walked back to Sam's place through the park. Ian took the couch, and I passed out on the floor. I could be happy with a bed. Could be happy with pancakes for breakfast. Even though music was the most spectacularly beautiful thing I'd ever done, I could abandon it. Jettison it on some country road. Leave it for dead beside a desert highway. It's me or it. Me or it. Me.

It.

Chapter 9

When I woke up the next morning, Sam, Ronnie, and Ian were already eating breakfast in the dining room. My leg was asleep, so it took me a minute to join them. They'd made eggs, pancakes, and bacon, and were washing it down with Stella Artois. Sam grabbed me a plate and a brew when I sat down.

"Sounds like you guys had a rough night," Ronnie said. Instead of beer, she was sipping a glass of tequila.

"Wasn't too bad," Ian said.

"I could hear ya snorin' like lumberjacks," she said. "I'll betchu were tired. Me, I'm not much of a sleeper, but who needs sleep when ya got blow, right?"

Sam popped *Off the Wall* in the record player and played "Don't Stop 'Til You Get Enough."

"Now, this is the way to start a day." Ronnie pulled me up to dance with her. I wasn't much of a dancer and tried to keep up with her while focusing on all of Sam's records on the shelves behind the table. The Dead, Dylan, Miles Davis, Hendrix, but also Phish, Radiohead, Pearl Jam, and Blur. Sam was one of those older cats who kept current with music.

"Doesn't he look like he's a having a seizure or something?" Ian said about me.

"Who cares how ya look? It's all about how ya feel," Ronnie said. She let go of me and snorted a few lines at the table. "And I'm feelin' good! Who wants somma this?"

Sam got up and did a line, but Ian and I refused. After breakfast, I forced myself to bring my plate to the sink and wash it. Something about chores felt as impossible as showering. Shit just got dirty again soon after, and cleaning took so much effort. But I put in the effort, thankful that Sam was letting us crash at his place, drink his beer, and eat his food.

"Let's hit the town!" Ronnie said.

"Okay," I said.

"I've gotta run some glass over to the Gladstone, or I'd come," Sam said.

"Don't worry about it," Ian said. "We'll catch up later for dinner."

It was a warm, sunny morning, but I grabbed a hoodie just in case the fog set back in, then followed Ronnie and Ian out the door. We headed east and stopped in every other bar we passed to do shots. By the time we reached the bay, I was plastered. Ronnie kept going on and on about some homeless guy who, "fucks like Genghis Khan. I swear, he's balled every one of my friends, and they all beg him for more. He's got a hog like a Hell's Angel, and I sucked that thing 'til my jaw burned."

We kept going until we hit the stadium where the Giants played. We passed the statue of Willie Mays and popped into a nearby dive. We ordered more shots, and Sam showed up about a half hour later. I was straight drunk when he arrived. I switched to beer to slow it down, and we shot some pool. Ronnie was a fucking tank. She kept tipping back tequilas, and I kept thinking we'd have to drag her out of there, but she just kept going, dancing around and singing every song that came on the jukebox. There was a guy dressed in business casual clothing sitting at the bar and mouthing the words to "Ripple." Something about the look on his face told me he knew what was good, but seeing those clothes on him looked all wrong. Dude had probably been a Dead Head at some point, but now he was just like everyone else. He was probably wealthy. He was probably happy. Was Sam happy? Or Ronnie? They both smiled a lot. But were they happy? Were they my future? Did I even have a future? Or was I the guy at the bar, putting quarters in the dive jukebox and playing songs off *American Beauty* while sipping top-shelf whiskey? In the short time I'd been there, it already seemed to me that the business casual dude represented all of San Francisco. That Sam and Ronnie were a dying breed, and when they were gone, that was it. I felt a tremendous pressure on my shoulders.

Ronnie handed us more shots, and I took another down. It started to come back up, but I took some deep breaths and held it in. For dinner we went to a fish place near the bay, and Ian and I shared the cheapest dish they had. We squeezed into Sam's truck and drove back to the guts of San Fran. He parked a few blocks from his place, and we walked the rest of the way, passing a street littered with homeless kids. They played bongos and sang off-key and mouthed off to passersby. One kid about my age played a guitar with the words "My other guitar is a syringe" written on it in black marker. That one got to me.

They reached out for us and begged us for change and told us we were bitches and all that crap, and I did everything I could not to let them touch me. Not to be swayed by their siren song, and as Sam unlocked and opened the door, all I could picture was Jerry Garcia's dead body lying in Buena Vista Park surrounded by yuppies taking pictures—close-ups of the syringe hanging out of his arm—and selling them as "art." This wasn't the Summer of Love. The Summer of Love was dead. No, this was the Summer of Crud, and it was layered so heavily all over me no amount of scrubbing would ever wash it off.

I woke up on the floor the next morning. Ronnie and Ian were in the dining room eating breakfast and listening to *Quadrophenia*. I started reading a small book on the Rolling Stones that I found under the couch and pretended to still be sleeping when Ian called my name. They were laughing louder and louder, and I could hear the clanging of the bottles as they set them down, so I figured now might be a good time to try. It was such a fucking gamble anyway.

I got up and walked quietly down the hall to the bathroom. The bathroom door didn't have a lock. Regardless, I unbuttoned and pulled down my pants as I neared the toilet. I wanted to put TP on the seat, but there was no time. The feeling could leave at any moment. Just sit and squeeze. The laughing continued in the dining room, relaxing me enough to sneak one past. This one was painful as hell—probably from all the walking the previous day—and there was a shitload of blood. I held a piece of TP in my ass and then took a look at it just as Ronnie busted in—no knocking or anything. "Yeah, they fuckin' rock—oh shit!" She looked at the TP in my hands, but instead of leaving, stood there and made conversation as if we were sitting at the dinner table. "Christ, I think it's baby's first period. I haven't seen that kind of blood in years. I'm all dried up like the Sahara now. Probably all the blow." Ian said something, and she shut the door and walked down the hall. I could hear her say, "He's giving birth in there."

I dropped the TP into the toilet while staring at a pair of electronic hair clippers in an open cabinet. I wiped up as much of the blood as I could, then joined Ian and Ronnie in the dining room. We had some beers and Ronnie belted out "Love, Reign o'er Me," then we took off for a party in the Castro. We stopped at a white Victorian house, and instead of knocking, Ronnie crowed like a rooster. A large bald dude with a goatee opened the door, snorting like a pig, and they hugged. Inside there were about fifteen to twenty people who looked to be in their late thirties to early forties. Two guys in the kitchen were brewing their own beer while some girls smoked grass at the table. The moment each of them saw Ronnie, they all started making animal noises, and it was soon clear that they each had their own unique sound. A guy with dreads handed me a stein filled with a homemade brew that was "infused with weed, man," and the girls let us get in on their circle.

The living room was filled with musical instruments, and I found myself instinctively wandering over. There was a sick Les Paul in the corner in front of a Marshall amp, and I wanted to plug in, turn it up to eleven, ring an E minor, and bring the whole house to the ground. The energy of the party started to follow me, and soon the five guys who lived in the house, who also played in a jam band together, each picked up their instruments and started to rock. And they were fucking tight—way tighter than we'd ever been. They built their song on the rhythm guitarist's harmony, a variety of jazzy chords, and the bassist worked the whole neck. The drummer had a second kit, and when he gave Ian the nod to hop on, Ian found the groove and worked it. That Les Paul in the corner still called me, but I got no nod. You can't just touch someone's guitar. That shit's sacred. Everyone started to gather around and the energy of the room was lifting. Still, maybe you got a nod and didn't see? Go pick it up. I mean, Hendrix would just walk over, unzip his pants, slap his nine-incher against the strings, and the whole world would cum all at once.

But you ain't Hendrix, homie. No, they'll beat your ass. They'll chase you right outta San Fran and back up into the mountains. I couldn't keep up with these guys anyway. The lead guitarist was rippin' it to shreds. A combination of soul and flawless technique. This is it, man. This is everything. This is how it all goes. Don't fight it. Just watch. Just tap your foot along. Just tap, you bitch. Charlatan. Your hair can't save you now. Nobody gives a fuck that you haven't showered in days. Nobody cares how much grass you've smoked. Nobody cares that you've smoked opium or taken shrooms. How many chicks you've fucked. How much shit you've smashed. Even if you shot H, you'd still be a fuckin' hack. The spotlight came upon you and you walked back to the shadows. Stop tapping your foot, you fucking piece of shit. Music doesn't give a shit how you look or smell. It belongs to the pure. It belongs to the strong.

After the party, we all went to a bar on Haight Street. Despite the crowd, we were able to get a big booth in the back. The place had a great vibe: paintings by local artists covered the walls and a band played the blues in the other room. I sat somewhere in the middle of the group, and the guy next to me pulled a growler out from under his hoodie and started pouring home brews for us under the table. He gave me one, and I sipped it while they all discussed some modern art movement going on in the area. I wished the band was in the same room as us, but they weren't, so I had nowhere to rest my eyes. With a band there, at least I had an excuse not to talk to anyone. I could never keep up in these types of conversations. I never had anything to say. I knew nothing about art or film or politics. I did, however, know about rot. I knew about pain. I knew about scabies and fear and insanity. I knew how to talk my way out of an ass-beating. There were fewer people seated to my left than to my right, so I thought about asking them to get out so I could use the bathroom, but I decided to slide under the table and crawl to freedom. The air started to get thicker in the bar, so I went outside and sat in the alley with my back to the wall. A homeless guy crawled out of the shadows and sat beside me. He said he'd once seen Gregory Corso and Michael McClure chatting in that same alley and sharing a jug of wine. He said that times were changing. He said the yuppies were winning. He said there was no pure place left in this world except that very alley. That this was the spot where they'd all leave us alone. I closed my eyes and opened them hours later when one of the two middle-aged women jogging by together stuck a ten-dollar bill in my hand. "These poor kids. Nobody's taking care of them." I thought about chasing her down and throwing the bill in her face and shouting, "I'm a teacher! A *teacher!*" but I crumpled it up and put it in my pocket. I got up and staggered back to Sam's place just as the sun had entirely risen.

Sam and Ronnie were in the kitchen blowing coke and singing along to Roberta Flack's "Killing Me Softly," and Ian was passed out on the couch. I went to the bathroom and pissed, then took a long look at myself in the mirror. I grabbed the hair trimmers and shaved my head as tears streamed down my face. I grabbed my hair out of the sink, threw it in the garbage, and took a shower. The water stung my ass so badly I almost screamed, but I deserved it. I toweled off, put my dirty clothes back on, and walked to the living room. When I passed the kitchen, Sam jumped and drew a gun on me. "Oh, sorry, Larry. Thought you were an intruder or something." He put the gun down.

"You gotta relax, Sammy," Ronnie said. She rubbed my head. "Ya kinda got the military thing goin' on now, but it's cool—I'd still suck your dick. It's like a commando-slash-hippy thing—kinda like the glue holdin' all this shit together or something, man. The yin and the yang. It's like, godly or something, ya know? I see you better now. You're like, a true artist. I see it, and I like it."

I passed out on the floor and woke up to Ian standing over me, pointing and laughing in my face. I put on a hat and ate some breakfast, then Ian and I grabbed our shit, thanked Sam and Ronnie, and took off.

"Bye, Harry! Bye, Ian! Tell your mother I miss her!"

We were staying in San Fran another night but didn't want to impose on them any longer. We drove to a posher neighborhood, dropped the car off at a mechanic who gave Ian a pretty good price on the brakes, and strolled up to a beautiful house on a hill overlooking the city. The beauty of it all strangled my mind. Ian knocked and a well-groomed man wearing an oxford button-down tucked into a pair of ironed blue jeans answered.

"Ian! I'm so glad you had the time to visit."

"No problem! I'm glad you invited us over."

"Your mother is practically family, which means you're practically family. Come in, come in."

Ian introduced us. His name was Ramon, and he complimented my hair. "Simple is highly underrated and always classy." He turned to Ian. "So, how's your mother doing?"

"She's thinking of retiring soon. She's been working at the hospital for over twenty years now, and she thinks it's time. Can't stand any more blood."

"I don't blame her."

Ramon's house had a simple, clean, and elegant modern design with a great view of the city. His son, Carlos, who was a year younger than I was, came home while we were eating grilled cheese sandwiches and tomato soup at the dining room table. Carlos was a lot like his father: well groomed, polite, and intelligent. He'd just finished a jazz piano lesson and was still jonesing to play some music, so we all went to the garage, which was filled with instruments, and had a jam session. I played an acoustic guitar, Ian an acoustic bass, Ramon an electric guitar, and Carlos played keys. After a few songs, Ramon pulled out some old music books and taught us the opening chords to Diana Ross's "I'm Coming Out." It wasn't that the song was all that difficult, it was just seeing all those seventh chords and quick changes made me realize pop music could also have value. Christ, I'd been shitting on pop tunes for years, but this was more complex than anything

I'd ever written. By the time we'd worked through the whole song, I realized I'd made the right decision with my hair.

Carlos, Ian, and I picked up the car and Carlos took us downtown to his favorite boba tea place, then to his favorite spot for sourdough bread. I didn't like either. We got some wine at a jazz bar, then went back to the house. Ramon had offered to let us spend the night, but neither Ian nor I felt comfortable with that, so we drove to the bay, smoked a joint, and passed out in the car while listening to Doug Morricone's CD on repeat.

Chapter 10

The Camry chugged over some dusty mountains, and on the other side, like a bright, shining bear trap, stood Los Angeles. San Francisco had been a bust, but maybe LA could still save me? Though I'd never been there before, I already knew that betting it all on LA was a surefire route to misery. Still, there was something about the city that reinvigorated me. San Fran had been gloomy and cool, but LA was bright and hot and sparkled like gold teeth. There was an energy here that, if I could learn to vibe with it, could potentially lift me up to the heavens. San Francisco was about art. LA was about making it big. This city was already full of wealthy charlatans. What was one more?

We got off the 5 in Glendale, found Billy's apartment complex, and knocked on his door. Billy had been in Ian's geology program at Conesus but was now working as a barista.

"Holy shit! You guys made it!" he said.

"Yeah, it was a long drive, and California's hot as fuck," Ian said.

"Well, come in, fellas, we're just getting the party started." He opened the door, and we walked in. For a three-guy apartment, it was actually pretty neat—other than the empties and bong on the coffee table and the massive drum kit behind the couch. Billy introduced us to his roommate Ivan, whom we didn't know but had grown up with Billy in Rochester and graduated the year before us. The other guy, Steve, had also been in Ian's geology program, and I'd blazed with him on a number of occasions. He hit me with the "Damn, you're looking like a Marine now" line when I said hi. There were a few other guys there too, and Ian and I set down our bags and started drinking with them. Someone popped in *Swingers*, and we watched it while passing the bong and pounding cans of PBR. When the movie finished, Ivan had the great idea to "Head to the fuckin' Dresden, man! I know the bouncer tonight. . . ." We got in three separate cars and drove over. At the door, Ivan said to us, "All right, guys, now just act cool," as if there was a chance they wouldn't let us in otherwise. We flashed our IDs and walked inside. It was busy, but not packed, and we sat at a booth. A cute barmaid brought us drinks, and I fought the urge to pass out on the table. The trip had been grueling, and it was starting to get to me. Ivan and Steve kept pointing at each other and calling each other "baby," and I couldn't take much more of it. I was grateful when they decided to call it an early night. When we got back to Billy's place, I passed out on one couch and Ian took the other, and I woke up around one the next afternoon.

Ian was in the kitchen arguing with his mom on the phone, and the other guys were at work, so I decided now would be the best time to try. But the second it started coming out, Ivan knocked on the bathroom door. "Oh, uh,

I thought you guys were gone. Gimme a minute." It started to work its way back inside, but I pushed with everything I had and won the battle. The bathroom was hot as fuck, and I was pouring sweat. I wiped as quickly as I could without causing any more damage, washed my hands, dried my face, and went back to the living room with a fire in my ass.

"Dude, what the *fuck* did you do to that couch?" Ian smirked as he pointed to a drool stain on one of the cushions. "Yo, Ivan just saw that shit, and he's pissed. He said this couch is an antique and that you just ruined it."

"Christ, it's a fucking couch."

"He looked like he wanted to beat your ass."

"I'll clean it."

"You better."

I wet a kitchen towel and scrubbed the stain.

"And what the fuck were you doing in there so long? You do realize there's only one bathroom here. Ivan said he's gonna be late for work now."

"I . . . I thought he was gone already." I started sweating again, hard. I wiped my forehead with the dry part of the towel.

"These guys are nice enough to let us stay here. Don't fuck up their shit."

"Well, then, let's switch couches tonight."

"Fuck that. You're sleeping on the floor."

Ivan came out of the bathroom, said nothing about the stain, and left for work. Ian stuck *Mulholland Drive* in the DVD player, and every ten minutes or so he'd say, "I bet you don't even get it." When the film was over, we popped in *Lords of Dogtown* and started passing the bong. After that, we watched *Falling Down*, and then my favorite film, *The*

Doors. When the guys got back from work, we ordered a pizza, drank a shitload of beer, and I passed out on the floor.

Despite the previous day's disaster with the bathroom, the next morning I decided to try to take a shower. Ian was rocking the drum kit, and I'd double-checked to make sure the other guys had gone to work, so I figured I was good. I took a quick shower, dried myself with the hand towel by the sink, put my dirty clothes back on, and went out to the living room. I ripped the bong a few times, pulled out my guitar, and started jamming with Ian. But the second I found a groove, he stopped.

"Yo, Luke Freemont is coming over," he said.

"He lives out here?"

"Yeah, he's down in East LA. He's comin' by to jam with me."

"Cool."

An hour later, Luke knocked on the door, shouting, "Excuse me, excuse me, is this the chronic masturbators support group? I had another incident on the bus over."

Ian laughed as he opened the door. "Dude, you're gonna get my buddy Billy evicted."

Luke had gone to high school with us in North Buffalo. He was a smart kid but had spent most of his teens dropping acid, and now there was something about him that was a little off. He never went to college—just spent his time playing with different bands and studying music independently. He was big into jazz, and he fucking killed it on drums. He was way more technically proficient than Matt, and he had that special "something" that made the music swing.

Ian relinquished the seat at the drums to its rightful

owner, then went to the kitchen to make some food. I grabbed my guitar and played a simple chord progression, and Luke took it to the next level. His rhythm opened me up in a way that had been closed for too long, and all of a sudden I started to feel it again. Holy shit! "Driv-in' through-the des-ert fee-ling brave. Driv-in' through-the des-ert fee-ling brave." Christ, that was it! That was the melody I'd been searching for, and it rushed through me like a herd of wildebeests. I could feel more of it coming. "A-flash up-on the-sand your-face turns-pale." It kept building. The chorus was coming. The heavens were opening. I could feel climax building up through me. "You were rock-in', but now you're—"

"Yo, Dumbass Dan, you used the last of the ketchup, didn't you?" Ian shouted from the kitchen.

No! No! No! Don't go! Come back! I tried to grab it, but like everything else, it slipped right through. For the love of fucking god, Ian, you used to lift me up! You used to lift me the fuck up!

The song was gone. I felt even more constipated than ever before. I thought about taking a dry dive out the fourth-floor window, but I just put the guitar away, went into the kitchen, and made a sandwich. Luke continued to play as if I'd never stopped. The dude had the groove and nothing would ever stop it. Nothing could end him. I grabbed the empty bottle of ketchup and threw it in the trash.

Luke eventually came over. "Hey, man, why'd you put your guitar away? That song you were singing was fucking amazing. That yours?"

I looked at Ian. "No."

"That's too bad. Man, whoever wrote that's a lucky bastard. I wish I could write tunes like that."

"Yeah, me too," I said.

When the guys came back from work, we brought our instruments outside and had a jam session. We took requests from passersby, which included "Patience" by Guns N' Roses to "Jane Says" by Jane's Addiction.

The guys knew of a party that night in Manhattan Beach, so we put the instruments away, piled into a few cars, and took off. The sun was just starting to set, casting the city in magic-hour lighting. The houses and palms reminded me of growing up in Florida. Reminded me of happier times. Without all the screaming and smashing. Without all the Evil Thoughts.

We arrived at a small beachside house just after sunset. We were the first guests to show up, and the owner of the house gave us a tour. Downstairs was the garage and upstairs was the house. The place was clean and stylish, and I overheard the owner tell Ivan that it "only costs nine hundred a month." *Only* nine hundred? Christ. To me, it might as well have been nine million. Just after graduating high school, I'd had such a bad panic attack while working at Taco Bell that I locked myself in the bathroom and pretended to be spray shitting until I felt sane enough to ask to go home. I couldn't even handle Taco Bell. How could I handle a job that paid enough to afford a place like this? Even the alley out back was out of the question. The cops would haul my ass away so fast, I wouldn't even be able to pop the top off my beer. The End was coming soon. Fall was coming soon. All I had left was this summer. I pounded some whiskey and followed the others out to the back deck overlooking the ocean, but they all started talking and laughing so I had to think fast. I saw a keg in the back corner. Keg stands are socially acceptable, right? I mean, frat dipshits smile and point at kegs and ask their "brothers," "Hey, who wants to do a keg stand?" while everyone smiles and laughs and cheers. Even though the others here were talking about geothermal energy or watersheds or some other important-sounding shit, they all started laughing and cheering when I asked them, "Hey, who wants to do a keg stand?" while I smiled and pointed to the keg in the back corner. I understood keg stands, and we hoisted each other up and chugged beer and screamed as the others started to arrive, and maybe, just maybe, they didn't all see how fucking weird and stupid I was.

The party got wild. There were hip sexy people everywhere, all groomed and painted and waxed to perfection. I was in my sweaty red gym shorts and a T-shirt and nobody'd want to talk with me beyond the radius of the keg's hose, so that's where I stayed for a while, shouting and cheering and holding people up to chug beer and share each other's spit. Hell, if they did want to talk to me, I wouldn't even know what to say. "Oh, yeah, my therapist tells me I need to learn how to enjoy myself too. Want some blow?" "Oh, yeah, my agent's been riding my ass too. I just want to take a little break though. Is that so much to ask? Some *me* time?"

I saw a guitar in the living room, so I went over and started strumming it, and soon I had a small crowd surrounding me and making requests. I played some of the songs we rocked on the sidewalk earlier that afternoon, and Ian and Luke came over and played the bongos. A cute girl kept smiling at me, but there must have been something wrong with her, so I disappeared onto the beach and pounded whiskey. But I knew from experience not to wander too far, or I'd end up on that beach forever while Ian continued down to Mexico with all my shit.

On my way back to the party, I saw Ian talking with a pretty girl. He had a way about him that attracted people, even when he was pissing all over them. For whatever reason, girls used to swarm him in college. He showered as infrequently as I did and never combed his wild hair. I knew we both stunk. We both hated the very people we tried so hard to impress. We pushed away the very people we wished we could call friends. I knew he wanted to belong—maybe more so than I did. He'd fight to the death to deny it, but he wanted to be part of the "cool group" more than anyone. But I think we both had a fucked-up perspective on how to go about doing that. We figured it best to push everyone away. To scorn the whole world. To tell them all to fuck off while holding so tightly onto this idea of purity—hoping they'd all see that we were on this quest for purity and realize how "cool" we were, then flock to us. Did that make us the biggest phonies of all?

I knew Ian would sell me out in a minute over a girl. Hell, he'd sell me out in a minute just to make the punch line to a shitty joke. Why did I even talk to him? What drew me to him? And him to me? He had a lot of other friends, but he hadn't invited any of them on this trip. He knew a shitload of much better guitarists, but when Matt and Zach asked him to start a band, he came to me first. He had much bigger friends, but when he wanted to take on the soccer team, he brought me.

But he treated me worse than any of them. With them, he smiled and charmed and swooned. I think he absorbed a lot of dark energy doing that shit, and he dumped it all over me. And for some sick reason, it made me feel special that he'd chosen me for this. That I was the one who really saw him. Saw him at his worst. I was his protector. The world's protector. A battered housewife. An abused child. The Darkness was addicting. There was ecstasy in depression. Honor in anxiety. I knew I was a sacrifice. And I knew so few of those others could handle such a role. My body was a host for scabies. My soul a portal to hell. But I knew that someday, because of all the horrors I'd seen, I would be able to save us all. How could I stomach conversations about fashion? How could I talk about internships and job interviews? They thought I was dirty. They thought I was weak. I was stronger than any of them; I was holding up the weight of the world.

Chapter 11

The next morning, Ian and I met Luke at Griffith Park. We played some Frisbee, then went for tacos. After, we cruised down Sunset Boulevard on our way to the beach, and Luke pointed out the record store where he worked. It was across the street from the Viper Room, where he said his band was gonna be jamming in a few weeks. A BMW pulled up next to us at a red light, and I could have sworn Halle Berry was behind the wheel. Later, I'd tell my friends that I proposed to her and she gave me an "Oh, you!" laugh then drove away, but in reality, I hid my face behind my hand and stayed like that for several blocks.

We arrived in Santa Monica and cruised along the beach, which was way too crowded for my liking. We walked along Venice Beach, taking in the freak show, then dropped off Luke at his place and headed back to Glendale. We grabbed our stuff, said goodbye to Billy and the others, and headed east through the desert.

It was hot as fuck in Barstow, even though the sun had already started to drop. When we stopped for gas, I checked a thermometer on the side of the pump, and it read a hundred and seven. Fuck. Even when the sun dropped, we couldn't escape the heat. Just kept driving deeper and deeper into its heart. By the time we arrived in Vegas, it felt as if nature had finally turned on us.

We cruised the main strip and took in the sights. There seemed to be a much higher proportion of assholes here than even in LA. Everyone was trying to outdo each other. Drivers revved their engines, people shouted shit. They all needed a good spanking (but not the kind advertised in the many fliers littering the streets). We took a right just before Circus Circus and drove for a few miles before pulling into the sprawling maze of an apartment complex that had far too few parking spaces. We found a spot on the street, grabbed our gear, and knocked on a few wrong doors before we found the right one.

Chad Harrington answered.

"Goddamn, I thought you guys'd gotten lost or something," he said.

"Easy to get lost in this monstrosity. They pay you to live here or something?" Ian said.

"It's Vegas, man. The only comforts we need are padded seats in front of the slot machines and a steady supply of AC."

It was like a meat locker in there, but I found it a relief. My nuts were sweating off my body. Ian introduced us, and we shook hands. Chad had also grown up in North Buffalo but went to private school, so I'd never met him. Regardless, having heard so many of Ian's stories about the pranks they'd pulled in the neighborhood and Chad's weird sexual habits, I felt as though I already knew him. Apparently, Chad liked to dress up like a schoolgirl, then have a woman lift up his skirt and pound him in the ass with a vibrating dildo. He also loved to jerk off on specific fabrics, including a handmade scarf that Ian gave me once to use while snowboarding— though he didn't tell me about it until later. It was weird shit, but I was pretty weird too, so whatever.

"Hey, you guys gotta swing by the casino tonight. I'm working the bar and can get you free drinks."

"Really?" I said.

"Yeah, as many as you want. I run that shit."

He went to his room and left the door open while changing into his work clothes. While Ian hopped on the computer, I checked out the apartment. Chad had a huge flat-screen TV and shelves of shitty made-for-video DVDs: *Police Academy 12* and *Van Wilder XIII: Let's Get Even Wilder!*

When Chad came out of his room, he pointed to a glass jar on the coffee table filled with weed. "I don't even smoke. You guys can have it."

"Holy shit, thanks!" I said. There had to be more than half an ounce in there.

"All right, I'm gonna head out, but make sure you guys come tonight. It'll be best around two or three."

"Cool, we'll see you there," Ian said.

I was starving, so I pulled a can of soup from my backpack and searched the kitchen for a bowl to heat it in, but couldn't find one. In fact, I couldn't find any silverware or cups or dishes or anything. The only thing in the fridge were some packets of mustard.

"What the fuck's going on here?" I said.

"That's just Chad. He's a weird dude."

I peeled the label off the soup can and opened it with my pocketknife, then put the can directly on a burner. When the soup started bubbling, I turned off the heat, wrapped the can in a T-shirt, and drank the soup down. We smoked some herb and watched a movie, then walked over to the casino. Even at night, it was hot as shit—the thermometer at Chad's place said it was still over a hundred. When we got to the casino, we went to the bar, and even though there was no one else around, Chad handed us a bill after we'd ordered our drinks. "Sorry, fellas, but the boss is watching."

On the casino floor, we played roulette, which was about the only game I knew how to play. Red or black. Odd or even. Simple enough. I was running low on cash, so I stopped gambling after losing ten bucks betting on black. Ian, however, put a twenty on red and won. Then he put that on red again and won. He kept doubling his money until he'd turned that twenty into six hundred and forty bucks. Our cheers filled the nearly empty casino. Ian wanted to stop, but I told him not to. "Think about it—if you walk away now, you got enough cash to bring us to Mexico in style, but you put it all on thirty-two and win, we could fucking *buy* Mexico. That's like a trillion dollars." Sure enough, he listened to my stoned ass, put it all on thirty-two, and lost it all. "When you think about it, you really only lost twenty bucks."

We went to an all-you-can-eat buffet, and I paid for Ian's food to make it up to him. We filled up on several plates of pasta and beans and rice and mashed potatoes. I got some of each animal, and we didn't stop eating until we were sweating and having trouble breathing. Ian ripped a heinous fart, and the couple next to us moved away, and we couldn't stop laughing.

"How much you wanna bet Chad just bought that herb to impress us?" Ian said.

"Whaddya mean?"

"I mean, I know the dude, and I wouldn't be surprised if he was just trying to make himself look cool."

"Either way, it works out for us." I was still ripped as fuck.

As we made our way to the exit, we stared at all the lights and shiny machines, then strolled back to the apartment. I picked up an escort ad to maybe jerk off to after Ian went to sleep, but ultimately figured fuck it and tossed it back on the ground.

When we got back, we smoked some more herb and fell asleep watching another shitty movie. Ian took the couch and I got the floor, but the carpet was soft and well padded, so it wasn't too bad.

I woke up around three p.m., but since Ian was still asleep and Chad was moving around the apartment, I kept my eyes closed. When Ian got up, so did I.

"Sorry about last night, fellas." Chad took a bite of some leftover pad thai in a Styrofoam container. "It's just my boss can be kind of a prick sometimes."

"This fucker made me lose over a thousand bucks last night," Ian said of me. "Woulda been better to have blown that cash at the bar. At least I woulda gotten something out of it." Ian opened Chad's laptop again and started clicking around.

"Hey, you're the one who put it all down," I said.

"Yeah, 'cause you kept telling me you had a feeling about that number. But it's just like everything else about you. Bullshit." Ian clicked some more. "What's your password for your online bank account?"

"Why?" I said.

"Yo, he's always like this," Ian told Chad.

Chad snickered. "You two bicker like a coupla bitches."

"C'mon, man, what the fuck you think I'm gonna do with it? I just wanna check how much cash you have left. Do you even know?"

Someone knocked at the door, and Chad went to answer it.

"Why do you care how much cash I have left?"

Chad gave the person at the door a warm welcome and let him in. "Hey, guys, this is my friend Christopher. Chris, this is Ian and Danny."

"Hi, boys," Christopher said.

"Hey," Ian said.

"Nice to meet you," I said.

"Oh, a Marine. I just love a boy in uniform. Where's yours?" he said, then winked at me.

"He'll put it on for you later," Ian said.

"Fuck you, man," I said. With hair, I'm Jim Morrison; without hair, I'm a Marine. With hair, I'm Jim Morrison; without hair, I'm a Marine.

"Yo, this dude's actin' all weird 'cause I asked him what his bank password is. What the fuck could I possibly do with it?"

"It's . . . it's the name of my dog, Samantha, and the day she died, five, five, zero, four."

Ian typed it in. "See? Wasn't so hard." He scanned the screen and started laughing.

"What?"

"Dude, you've got like twenty bucks left."

"You gotta be kidding me."

"Naw, man, you blew it all."

"What am I gonna do?"

"Fuck if I know. Maybe you can blow dudes down on the strip for nickels."

"I've got plenty of change in my car," Christopher said.

"Fuck you guys," I said. I got up and went to the bathroom. When I came out about twenty minutes later, the guys were arguing in the living room.

"No way, she can fucking *sing*," Chad said.

"Ask him," Ian said to Christopher.

"Ask me what?" I said.

"Lindsay Lohan or Britney Spears?" Christopher said.

"Lindsay Lohan or Britney Spears what?" I said.

"Please, everyone falls somewhere between the two. Which do you gravitate more toward?"

"That's gotta be one of the dumbest things I've ever heard," I said.

"Naw, man, it's actually pretty brilliant when you think about it," Ian said.

"Don't think," Christopher said. "Just answer."

"Uh, Lindsay Lohan?"

They all laughed.

"What?"

We smoked a shitload of pot, then piled into Christopher's Jeep Wrangler, which had the top off, and Chris blasted "Wake Me Up Before You Go-Go" as we cruised down the strip. Ian, Chad, and I kept shouting "Orange Mocha Frappuccino!" at people we passed. Some smiled. Others told us to fuck off.

We hit a few casinos, then some bars, but I didn't buy shit. I had my flask, and it did me good. Somewhere along the way I got separated from the group and stopped in a karaoke bar. I sipped a bottle of their cheapest brew while a drag queen brought the house down belting out Chaka Khan tunes. She fucking dominated the stage. The place was packed and everyone was cheering her on. I sat in the back corner and studied her movements. Her voice. How she controlled the stage. How the people adored her.

After a few songs, she got off the stage, and some dipshit Middle-American-looking man butchered a Hank Williams tune, so I left and staggered up the hot, dusty road. Scattered below me were more fliers of beautiful women just dying to fuck me for my last ten bucks. "C'mon, big boy. I love a man who serves his country." With hair, I'm Jim Morrison; without hair, I'm a Marine. With hair, I'm Jim Morrison; without hair, I'm a Marine. Above me, the golden sun was just beginning to rise, filling the desert horizon with deep purples and yellows and reds. I looked around at all the strip clubs and seedy bars and sick fuckers looking for their fixes. Then I looked back up at that quiet, confident sunrise. Even here, nature was winning.

After a nearly three-mile, blazing-desert walk, I arrived at the maze of the apartment complex. I followed my instincts and somehow found the right place. Chad and Christopher were giggling in the bedroom, and Ian was sprawled on the couch. I snuck off to the bathroom, closed the door quietly, squeezed the life outta me, and wiped the sweat away with a towel. There was no TP, so I used some paper towels I found in the trash. Not too much blood this time. I lay on the floor by the sliding glass door, checked the thermometer—ninety-nine degrees—and fell asleep. I was a desert Marine. A desert Marine.

I woke up around five to Chad bitching to Ian about his ex-girlfriend. "Yeah, and you'll never believe this. Early one morning, I saw her sneaking out of the bathroom, and she jumped when she saw me. When I started walking toward the bathroom, she pleaded with me not to go in, but I just laughed at her and went in anyways. She fucking tore the place up. While I was pissing, I started thinking, and it hit me: I never once saw her shit. She must have done that every morning—wake up super early so she could sneak one in before I got up."

Holy shit! What did he know?

Chad went to work, and Ian and I smoked the rest of the weed, then walked down to the strip. About halfway there, I slipped on one of the whore ads on the sidewalk and almost fell. Ian laughed.

"Watch it, Manger-birth Wolinski," he said.

"What the fuck are you talking about?"

"You don't remember?"

"Remember what?"

"Dude, at one of our shows you stopped playing and started shouting shit like 'Manger Birth!' and 'Webbed Toes!' into the microphone."

"Really?"

"Yeah, man. People started looking at you like you were crazy. But I thought it was pretty cool."

We walked a little farther up the street, and I said to him, "Thanks for telling me that, Quick-shitter Perez."

Ian laughed.

I didn't realize how stoned I was until we got to the strip. All the lights and bells and whistles and people screaming shit. We went to Circus Circus and my senses were overwhelmed, but I was all right. There's no way Paul Bern could have handled this. Paul Bern's brain would've snapped the second he walked in, and he'd start screaming like a maniac until security had to drag him out. And even so, he'd claw and fight his way back in. Maybe for nothing more than to prove to himself he could handle it. That he could make it. But you know what? Fuck Paul Bern. You're not Paul Bern. Paul Bern is weak. You're strong. You're still here, and none of these fuckers can do it. None can take you down. You're stronger than all of 'em. Who could endure what you have and still be here? Who could blaze across a country a hundred miles an hour without burning up? Coast to coast in moments? Life to life in seconds? All with a bleeding asshole and a knife in the gut? With a head full of dynamite and a heart churning like an ocean? You're better than all of 'em. You're strong. You're beautiful. When the world comes crashing down on us all, you'll be one of the only ones left standing. You'll be up there—finally where you belong. You'll be up there because of all this. This beautiful, lovely burden! You're a fuckin' superhero, Danny. You're gonna save the world someday. Someday, you're gonna save us all. Just not tonight. Just not tonight.

We left the casino and walked the strip. Some d-bags walked by, chanting and shouting and shit, and when one asked Ian where the real party was, I averted my gaze. Ian pointed somewhere in the distance, and they took off just as some chicks wearing sashes and tiaras came up the other way. A bachelorette party, probably. The guys and girls swirled together, and they took off for the spot Ian had told them about. I never knew whether he was actually sending people off someplace cool or if he was just fucking with them, but either way, those fuckers left us alone so they could go do what it was we all knew they were gonna do.

The walk back was hot as fuck. I spent my last four bucks on a burrito and hoped it'd fill me long into our trip through the Mexican desert.

We woke up around five p.m., gathered our shit, and said goodbye to Chad. I called my sister while I drove, and she said she would put a hundred bucks in my bank account tomorrow. The same sister I'd terrorized when I was a kid. And now, gimme, gimme, gimme, you ugly bitch! Gimme, or I'll rip your head off! Gimme, or I'll piss on you in your sleep!

The Arizona desert sky was one of the most magnificent sights I'd ever seen. A thunderstorm worked its way across the atmosphere just as the sun dipped below the mountains in the distance. The whole world was warm blues and purples with electricity zipping through. At Ian's suggestion, we pulled into a parking lot at the North Rim of the Grand Canyon. "It's less crowded than the South Rim and has the best views." But it was too dark to see anything, so we just slept in the car.

I woke early the next morning to a mother scolding her kid.

"I said don't run off!"

"But, Mommy, there's a trail."

"There's no trail."

"But I see it!"

I popped the Johnny Cash disc back in the CD player and played his cover of "I Hung My Head." Of all the songs we listened to on those roads, that's the one that most reminds me of our trip. The sun was just starting to rise and, through the trees, I could see small parts of the canyon here and there. But even with a limited view, I knew exactly what it looked like. Ian woke up.

"Let's go home," I said.

"Yeah."

I started up the car, backed out, and drove to the highway, and we rolled thirty hours straight home, stopping only for gas and to piss, rolling, rolling, rolling straight across the country, straight across the world, forever into the darkness, forever into oblivion.

About the Author

Jonathan LaPoma is an award-winning novelist, screenwriter, songwriter, and poet from Buffalo, NY. In 2005, he received a BA in history and a secondary education credential from the State University of New York at Geneseo, and he traveled extensively throughout the United States and Mexico after graduating. These experiences have become the inspiration for  much of his writing, which often explores themes of alienation and misery as human constructions that can be overcome through self-understanding and the acceptance of suffering.

LaPoma has written five novels, thirteen screenplays, and hundreds of songs and poems. His screenplays have won over 160 awards/honors at various international screenwriting competitions, and his black comedy script *Harm for the Holidays* was optioned by Warren Zide along with Wexlfish Pictures (*American Pie, Final Destination, The Big Hit*) in July 2017.

LaPoma's novels have been recommended by *Kirkus Reviews* and Barnes and Noble (B&N Press Presents list), have hit the #1 Amazon Bestseller lists in the "Satire," "Urban Life," "Metaphysical," "Metaphysical & Visionary," and "Religious &

Inspirational" Kindle categories (USA, Canada, and Australia), and have won awards/honors in the 2018 Eric Hoffer Book Award, the 2016 and 2017 Florida Authors and Publishers Association President's Awards, and the 2015 Stargazer Literary Prizes. He lives in Mexico City.

www.jonlapoma.com

Also by Jonathan LaPoma

Hammond, The Summer of Crud, Understanding the Alacrán, Developing Minds: An American Ghost Story, and *The Soul City Salvation* are books one-five of a loosely-linked series. Each novel can be read independently of the others.

Hammond
A group of troubled but charismatic boys in a tough Buffalo, NY neighborhood play basketball at a local park and dream winning a state high school championship.

The Summer of Crud
The summer after graduating from college, a mentally ill 22-year-old takes a cross-country US road trip with a friend, hoping to find the inspiration to reach his songwriting potential, start a band, and avoid student teaching in the fall.

Understanding the Alacrán
A 22-year-old man moves to Mexico and better understands the addiction and mental illness destroying his life.

Developing Minds: An American Ghost Story
A group of recent college graduates struggle with alienation and addiction as they try to survive a year of teaching at dysfunctional Miami public schools.

The Soul City Salvation
Not yet ready to take on Hollywood, a 26-year-old aspiring actor and writer moves to Soul City, CA and begins therapy for OCD, setting him on a ten-year healing journey that drives him to near madness as he explores the limits of his heart, creativity, and psyche.

A Noble Truth (screenplay)
Two friends set off on a road trip to explore what truths unite people in a modern America dominated by apathy and discord. It is soon clear, however, that truth is the last thing either man seeks.